INSIDE:

PERRON MANOR

LEE MOUNTFORD

FOREWORD

I am a man who has devoted his life to the study of the paranormal, and one who has travelled the length of our country in the pursuit of the truth. The idea that there is something beyond death is a notion that both consumes and drives me. I have-both on my own and with my team-investigated countless places and buildings that are said to be haunted. Most are not. A rare few, however, have offered up evidence and experiences that make what I do worthwhile. Whether others believe me or not, I have seen things to convince me that this mortal shell is not all there is to the thing we call 'life.' Or, more aptly, to existence.

Despite the many miles I have travelled in my studies, is it not strange—perhaps even fitting—that the most notorious and storied place of all is one that sits in my own home town of Alnmouth?

That building is Perron Manor. The Devil's House.

It was Perron Manor, along with its history and legends, that sparked my fascination with the supernatural at a very young age. Indeed, my step-sister and I used to stay up late most nights telling stories of undead things that roamed the creaking halls and corridors of the house.

The building has been many things during its long lifetime, and has known many names and served many functions: a home, a monastery, even a hotel. The building was known as The Blackwater Hotel in 1982, and that is a year that will long be remembered in Alnmouth, though undoubtedly a year many of the locals desperately want to forget.

The history of the building is quite extraordinary, and many tragedies have befallen the Manor. Some events are documented in official records, but others are remembered through the stories told by the locals of Alnmouth, and also through eyewitness accounts of those that have wandered too close to the property's grounds.

Frustratingly, it is a place now closed off to everyone other than its solitary warden: a person who has made it very clear that he does not want visitors anymore.

And that pains me.

Because, in 2013, my team and I were given access for two full nights. It was our one and only investigation there.

We weren't prepared.

Most genuinely haunted places are actually quite serene in truth, even if the entities there can get a little mischievous at times. Perron Manor is different. It is much more insidious and—I hesitate to use the word for fear of sounding cliché—evil than any other building I have been in. I could almost sense the harm the house wanted to do to me whilst there. And the things it showed us will stay with my team and me forever.

Which is why I so desperately want to go back.

That seems unlikely now—at least until Perron Manor changes hands again.

Nevertheless, given the building's history is so rich, and the eyewitness accounts so extraordinary, I felt it necessary someone chronicle exactly what has happened there over the years.

That is my intention with this book: a labour of love to a place that both fascinates and terrifies me.

So, dear reader, please turn the page if you are feeling brave enough. The house we are about to focus on, while not having nationwide recognition like some (which are usually faked, by the way), is one I can confidently state to be the most haunted and malevolent in the United Kingdom.

It is Perron Manor. The Devil's House. A place that evil calls home.

—*David Ritter, Paranormal Investigator, 2018.*

WHAT TO EXPECT

Before we dive into the history of the house we are here to investigate, I want to take a moment to outline the format this book will take, so you know what to expect.

The first section is what I call the early history of the house: from its construction in 1282, all the way up to the mid-nineteen hundreds. As you will have discovered in the Foreword, I have a strong interest in the house, and had studied it quite extensively already, even before the idea of this book ever entered my mind. This gave me quite the head start when I finally decided to turn my knowledge into a tome, as I was able to go back and take information from my existing and extensive notes. One thing I was therefore aware of, was just how sparse the information was for the early part of Perron Manor's existence. I redoubled my efforts when starting my writing, of course, to try and track down any documentation I could, but it proved difficult to find anything new. Therefore, the first section of the book might seem light in detail, especially considering the period of time involved. This is purely because, as should be quite obvious, we simply don't have much in the way of records to draw from, given their scarcity from those times. Still, I have found what I could, and I feel it both outlines the history of the building and leads up nicely to more recent events.

For these earlier years, what information I have found has come from a variety of sources. The first is a heritage centre in Northumberland, not far from the town of Alnmouth. And while I couldn't take any of the documents away with me, I was able to make in-depth notes, which I feel gives me a solid picture of what happened during these earlier years.

The internet was, obviously, a great help, but tricky in that much of the information was unverifiable, so I tried to use anything I found there sparingly.

Lastly, there was also a book written and published in 1976, by a gentleman named Oscar Simmons. It was called, *Perron Manor: A History of Blood*. This book is no longer in print, unfortunately, and almost impossible to get hold of. Fortunately for me, however, it is a book my father owned, as he'd bought it on a whim not long after its release. My father never did read the book, and it sat on a shelf collecting dust until I picked it up one day. I was already intrigued by the strange house in town, and was elated to find information on it so close at hand. I still have that book today, falling apart though it is, and much of what you read here in the first section is taken from *Perron Manor: A History of Blood*. Were Oscar Simmons still alive today, I would have personally thanked him, but he died shortly after the book's release. I have since learned the publisher went out of business, and the rights for the book have been forgotten, or lost. Hopefully, my book can help keep the work Oscar started alive for a little while longer. I tried to verify any claims made in Oscar's book where I could, and sometimes I was able to, but there are, of course, many occasions where that was not possible. In these cases, I am unable to confirm what Oscar's sources were, but that doesn't mean what he has written is incorrect. I made the decision to include any interesting details from his book even if I am unable to fully verify or cross-reference them, especially if I feel said information is of benefit to the reader.

The second section of the book moves on to the recent history of the house, and it focuses mainly (though not exclusively) on the events from 1982, when Perron Manor also gained the name The Devil's House. Given this was less than a lifetime ago, we have much more in the way of verifiable information to go on, so I need not go into too much detail here. However, as I can draw on more sources, and even eyewitness accounts, we are able to shape a much more solid and cohesive picture of this timeframe.

The last section is the most personal for me, and it will detail the investigation my team and I carried out in 2013. It was a two-night project, and what happened there will stay with me forever. Given I was present for all of it, we do not need any records or eyewitness accounts to verify anything. I just hope my words are enough to convince you that what I'm saying is true. Because it is.

Every word of it.

SECTION 1

The Early History

1

BARREN LAND

As promised, we will start at the beginning. To do that, we need to go way back, to before the first brick of Perron Manor was even laid. I'll take you to the year 1282.

We also need to travel to the far north of England, to the County of Northumberland, which lies close to the Scotland borders. Back then, the settlement now known as Alnmouth was non-existent, and the building that we know as Perron Manor was in its planning stages. It was to be a small monastery, built on an open area of grassland that sat between an enclave of trees shielding it from view. The spot was also relatively high in altitude, on the crest of a hill. In the summer of 1282, the building work began in earnest. Though no exact figures were given in the records I found, there was mention of an 'unusually high' number of deaths during the seven-year construction period. In addition, there was also a passage that described the construction crew having to disperse a group of strange nomads from the land before work began. These people 'did not speak the king's tongue, worshipped ungodly things, and were strange to look at.' (Please note the previous quote is a rough translation from Middle English.) Unfortunately, there was no further information on the natives.

When the building was finished in 1289, the area below the hill was quickly settled and a small village emerged.

As previously stated, the monastery was smaller than most, and was of a stone construction, with a slate-tiled roof. A grand double door in the centre of the front elevation was flanked on either side by windows, which continued up both stories of the building. The monastery was roughly square in shape, but arched heads to the windows and doors gave the building some additional character.

The building was initially intended to house only eight monks, and it is said all remained there until 1296, when all but one were killed. According to several accounts, they were murdered by the one and only survivor—the Mad Monk. Again, there is frustratingly little information on the event, but it just goes to show that tragedy and sinister events in the building are just as old as the structure itself. Perhaps those events are even older, given the mention of the strange tribe who inhabited the land before the monastery was built.

I had hoped to be able to find some information on the original architect of the building, or even some plans and blueprints, but my searches yielded no results. The best I have been able to find are some old artists' impressions of what the building originally looked like when it was constructed.

Records are scarce following the murders, and I could not find any information pertaining to the property again until the mid-thirteen hundreds.

2

EDWARD GREY

IT WAS the year 1356 when Edward Balliol surrendered his title as King of Scotland to Edward III. During that time, the former monastery was used as a stop-off to some of King Edward III's men: a place to stay as they marched to and from the Scottish borders. The building was, at that time, under the direct control of the crown, and its sizeable basement was converted into a dungeon, where captured enemy soldiers and even some deserters were brought back, imprisoned, and—when required—tortured. Exactly when the conversion took place is unclear, but the custodian during that time was Edward Grey, and the property was officially known as Grey House. While it is more than a little frustrating that I cannot pin down the exact date Edward Grey gained ownership, the events that took place in 1356 were very strange, and were the first in a series that took place under Grey's watch.

Indeed, it is apparent that Edward Grey himself was quite the insidious character, and perhaps even served a being other than the king.

The warden of Grey House is a man I have researched quite extensively due to my obsession with the building, and what I found was both interesting and disturbing.

For one, I discovered that in 1356 Edward Grey started to take an active role in the torture of any prisoners held at the house, and did so with relish and a sadistic glee. The average lifespan of anyone incarcerated there was a few weeks at best, and word got around; Grey House soon received a reputation similar to what we would today call a death-camp. It is not known why he became so involved with that side of things, especially given there were already people living at the grounds who were responsible for the prisoners and their 'wellbeing.' Whether Edward Grey had this sadistic streak before he came to the manor or if it was something he developed during his time there is unclear, but that side of his personality soon grew out of control.

In 1358 there was a report that recorded how one of the servants living at the building heard something strange in the dead of night. After venturing down to the dungeon, the man witnessed Edward Grey carrying out a horrific act upon the dead body of a prisoner, dismembering and rearranging limbs across the stone floor. Grey was kneeling in the centre of the arranged body parts, covered in blood while chanting in a tongue unknown to the eavesdropper.

It would seem that such incidents became more commonplace, as sometime in 1362 the staff and servants all abandoned Grey House, leaving only Edward and any remaining prisoners. No one else returned until the winter of that year, when a garrison was sent by the king to investigate. There, they found that Edward's activities had moved beyond the dungeon. Body parts were scattered throughout the house, hung on the walls or arranged in strange patterns on the floors, accompanied by odd markings drawn in blood and chalk. There was an overpowering smell of decay and death and Edward Grey was also found dead, swaying in the wind and hanging by his neck down the front face of the building. You would be forgiven for thinking this an obvious suicide, but when one looks at all the details, the assumption becomes less certain. For one, Edward Grey was dangling above the entrance door, and the rope around his neck was tied to an iron outcropping halfway up the external wall—not an easily accessible area. In addition, and more disturbing, was that his stomach had been pulled open, and his decayed, festering insides lay in a pile beneath him, just outside of the main entrance. His jaw, too, had been ripped off.

It seems impossible that these wounds were self-inflicted, meaning they were likely carried out after he was hung (given the mound of his own guts on the ground, as well as his jaw, lying beneath where Grey was hanging). So, it is likely that after being hung, someone—or some*thing*—carried out the disembowelment, possibly while Grey was still alive. What is unclear is whether the attacker was the one to initially hang Grey, or if they were merely some kind of sick opportunist who acted after a suicide.

Like many of the records from the house's earliest years, the lack of any great detail means conjecture is the only way to make sense of things. I acknowledge this is hardly scientific, especially when coming from the angle of the paranormal. After all, how can one remain impartial and objective if we jump to conclusions when there simply isn't enough information to connect the dots? That is a fair criticism, so we cannot say for certain the things that happened at the Manor during Edward Grey's stewardship were caused by anything other than a sick man's mind.

That, however, would discount the strange things that

happened after his death. Edward Grey's story is just one small part of the Perron Manor legacy, and therefore needs to be seen as part of the whole.

So, to help with that, we now venture forward to the turn of the fifteenth century.

3

SICK HOUSE

You will notice there are jumps in time between the periods I cover in this book. However, to be clear, I am not making the case the house had been inactive during the intervening years. Indeed, there could have been countless incidents of paranormal activity that we are simply unaware of due to the lack of recorded evidence. This is to be expected when looking back so far into history, of course.

My own inclination is to believe that Perron Manor has always been very much active, regardless of whether or not there is evidence. As you will see when we move forward through time, what records we *do* have show continued and consistent incidents, which I believe cannot solely be attributed to coincidence.

But, moving on, let us now look to the year 1408.

Though we do not know how it came to be so, in 1408 we see the first mention of the building being used as a sickhouse for the infirm and dying; the location served many nearby villages and towns—including Alnmouth. We can't be sure as to what sort of practices went on during this time, but it is noted that many patients and residents died under 'unclear' and 'unsavoury' circumstances. There is also a brief description in the book, *Perron Manor: A History of Blood* (which I made mention of earlier), sharing how strange people living in the woods made themselves known to the staff and residents of the infirmary. Could these be descendants of the folk who were 'strange to look at' in 1282, which we covered in Chapter 1? While we don't have much to go on, *Perron Manor: A History of Blood* does seem to imply that it is more than a mere coincidence. But who were those people? And how did a populace living within the woods go unnoticed for so long?

Perron Manor: A History of Blood also mentions the disappearance of a young boy, the son of one of the attendants who worked at the house. He went missing from his nearby home in Alnmouth, and some workers at the infirmary insist they had seen him roaming the halls shortly after. Despite thorough searches, the boy was never found. His mother, driven mad with grief, was told her services were no longer required. However, she kept returning to the manor, convinced her son was still there. She did this until her death, still swearing her son was at the house, and that she had seen him peering at her from the windows—as young as the day he went missing.

Others claim to have seen him throughout the years as well, though by their account the boy was indeed ageing; they detailed him appearing progressively worse as time went on, and one account describes his appearance as 'horribly decayed and rotted.' The boy's actual name was not given, so remains a mystery.

Another story tells of strange markings and symbols found scrawled and scratched into the walls and floors, but it is unclear as to who made them. In 1427, the building was closed as a sick-house, due to the 'constant outbreak of diseases,' and the doors were locked for over 150 years before the house came into the ownership of the esteemed Perron family. It is shocking to see how quickly esteem can turn into infamy.

4

PERRON MANOR

In 1579, Grey House was officially handed over to the Perron family, who were of noble lineage. Baron Perron was an officially recognised title in the Peerage of England, created specifically for the patriarch of the Perron family, Charles Perron. The former Grey House became the seat of the Perrons, and in 1579 it formally became known as Perron Manor—a place from which Charles Perron aimed to build his social standing.

Not long after moving in, Charles commissioned an extension to the rear of the building, with two wings running off the main structure, turning the footprint into a 'U' shape. He also added in a courtyard to the space between the new wings, and a new living level was created within the roof space, to increase the capacity of the building.

These changes gave the property an added feeling of grandeur, and hence was more fitting to its new name.

The first few years of the family's ownership seemed to pass without any incident of note, or at least any record of anything happening. In fact, the settlement of Alnmouth apparently prospered during the first ten years of the Perron family taking over. In the year 1590, however, there is a record of Charles Perron's mental state failing. As he got older, it was noted that he started to become extremely paranoid and delusional. Now, there is nothing to link the deterioration of his mental state to anything paranormal, of course, but some of the things he was reported to have said are very interesting—such as being adamant that there were 'others' living in the manor with the family, watching them in the night. He also claimed to have seen 'dead things coming out of the walls.' Fantastical stories, and definitely something that could be explained as a sick mind. However, given the history we have covered already, as well as what is to come, Charles' claims certainly warrant inclusion.

The health of the patriarch slumped further, and in the autumn of the year 1591 he passed away, though the cause of death is unknown. The house was then left to his firstborn son, Robert Perron.

5

ROBERT PERRON

ROBERT PERRON REMAINED at the Manor until his eventual death, living to the ripe old age of ninety-four. That is rare even by today's standards, but back then it was almost unheard of. His long life, and long tenure at Perron Manor, grew stranger with each year that passed.

Though not as widely known as people like Aleister Crowley, Robert Perron is, nevertheless, one of the earliest-known practitioners of the occult in the United Kingdom. It is not recorded when he became drawn to such dark arts, or how he became aware of them in the first place, but there is a passage in a journal from 1604—a letter written by the Earl of Suffolk—that references Perron Manor, and Robert Perron specifically.

Now, considering Suffolk is at the other side of the country from Perron Manor and Northumberland, the fact that this news travelled so far is interesting.

In the report, the Earl—Lord Thomas Howard—makes mention of troubling stories coming from the local villagers of Alnmouth. The stories told of strange, unholy practices taking place up at the Manor, and the local populous was growing frustrated and even frightened while living under the rule of the new Barron.

In 1613, it seems the occult interests of Robert Perron were perhaps reaching new heights. The book *Perron Manor: A History of Blood*, shows correspondence from an officer in the Northumberland branch of the Office of the Lord Lieutenant. In this letter, he tells of how many people in Alnmouth had gone missing. It was strongly rumoured those poor souls had been kidnapped and taken up to Perron Manor, where the Barron was indulging in practices that involved human sacrifice. The letter also showed that even though the author believed the rumours to be true, the powers-that-be did not want any investigation to take place into the Barron at that time.

This revelation immediately brings to mind Edward Grey. There are striking resemblances between the two men, specifically the kinds of acts they are alleged to have taken part in. Such atrocities, though hundreds of years apart, are too similar to be mere coincidence, at least in my view. It leads me to believe there may be a certain ancient 'force' at work both in the building and the land it is built on. This hypothesis is something that is only strengthened, I feel, as we move through the years.

As I have said before, the lack of any real detail or in-depth knowledge of the house's early history is frustrating, but particularly so during the time Robert Perron was the patriarch of the Manor. I believe this is one of the key periods of the building's existence, given how long Robert lived there. While there are stories, I feel that much of what really happened has been lost to time. One such example is the immediate family of Robert who lived in the Manor with him. It is known that he had two younger brothers and three younger sisters, and his mother also lived there with them for some time after the death of her husband, Charles. But there is precious little information regarding these family members, and it is unclear if they were involved in, or even comfortable with, Robert's practices.

We do know that his mother died in the year 1618, but we do not know the cause of death. Robert's siblings, all younger, also died off in the years that followed, concluding with his youngest sister, Lynn, dying in 1642. We also know that Robert did not marry or have children (at least, there is no record of it). Also, we cannot be sure if any of Robert's siblings bore children, but historical records state that Robert was the last surviving Perron family member; there were no heirs that could inherit the property after his death. It seems odd that there were no children between the six siblings.

Either no offspring were born, or there *were* descendants of the Perron bloodline who were never officially recognised.

Perron Manor became a place that was feared by the local village-folk, with tales of strange noises coming from the place in the dead of night: screams, chanting, and other sounds not so easily classified.

Robert Perron passed away in 1664. His cause of death is not known, but someone living until they were ninety-four is astonishing for the sixteen hundreds.

But it is what was discovered following Robert's death that was truly interesting: scores of bodies, all of different ages and in different states of decomposition, were found strewn around the house. Some were mounted or displayed in what were noted as 'deliberate' poses, while others were simply discarded. The basement, in particular, was reportedly 'ankle-deep with the dead.'

It was human sacrifice on a huge scale, but what Robert

Perron was trying to achieve with it will, unfortunately, never be known.

Following Robert's death, records on the Manor were limited up until the year 1762. Between 1664 and the mid 1700s, all I could deduce was that the property remained a home under private ownership. It seems the house did change hands a few times, though I have no information on how, why, or to whom.

In 1837, however, it becomes a little more clear, and records show that Perron Manor then became an orphanage.

6

ST. MARY'S ORPHANAGE

THANKFULLY, as we move into the eighteen hundreds, records become a little easier to locate and reference, and the history of Perron Manor more detailed.

A newspaper article in *The Northumberland Chronicle* shows us that St. Mary's Orphanage first opened its doors in October of 1837. Even though the report made it sound like a positive event, St. Mary's did not prove to be a nice place for these children to live in—not that any orphanage back in those days really would have been. St. Mary's, however, was a particularly difficult place for children to grow up. For one, in 1841, the same newspaper that announced the opening of the orphanage then ran a story of strange tales told by children who had escaped and fled. These children were, it said, terrified, and one of them relayed a tale of how 'horrible, frightening people' would come out of the walls for them; if the strangers caught any of the boys, they would drag the unfortunate victims back with them. The boy claimed that everyone who had been taken had previously confided in their friends that they'd woken in the night to find a pale-faced man standing at the end of their beds, watching them sleep.

Jumping to 1854, a report in a different paper states that 'Old Perron Manor is again extending its terrible legacy of tragedy as a spate of deaths half the numbers of both staff and residents.' It was put down to a cholera outbreak, but did note it was odd no other outbreaks or cases of the disease had been recorded during that time in the surrounding areas.

In 1862, there was a letter written by one of the staff at the institute, a woman only known as 'Liz,' which was never sent. It was addressed to someone named Anne. I have seen this letter in the Northumberland Historical Society, where it is displayed; though some of it is illegible, I was able to make out most of its contents. Liz was expressing her concern at living in the building, having started only a few months earlier. She said that many of the staff, especially the elders, were extremely 'cold and odd,' with no warmth to them. The children, too, were like 'brainwashed husks,' with only the newer residents showing any kind of emotion or personality. She then spoke of some 'strange and terrible things' she had experienced while there. It started out with odd noises in the night—someone banging on her door, even though no one was there when Liz checked—but then moved on to things much worse. Children went missing, and it seemed like the people who ran the facility showed little concern. Liz then said that she'd started to hear chanting in the night. One evening she went to check the dormitories, and was met with most of the kids screaming and terrified, with one of them now gone. Talk of 'the pale men coming to get them,' was the only explanation the children could give. The letter ended with Liz considering her future at the facility, but her ultimate fate is unknown.

St. Mary's Orphanage was eventually closed down, and a newspaper named *The Northern Echo* ran the following story on September 21, 1881:

Cursed Orphanage Closed Indefinitely:
On Saturday evening, police from Northumberland Constabulary entered St. Mary's Orphanage, unprepared for what they would find. Death. And its stench permeated the air.

Bodies of the poor children, as well as the staff, were found littered around the premises, with no one left alive. The dead were in a foul state, with ungodly acts committed upon them. It was also reported that the number of the deceased was curiously low, with many of the people living at the institute unaccounted for.

The troubled institute has had a history of tragedy. Now, after this latest and most severe of incidents, its doors are rumoured to be closed for good.

What will become of the notorious building, once known as Perron Manor, is uncertain, but many locals in Alnmouth think the cursed place should be burned to the ground.

A few years after the closure of St. Mary's Orphanage, in 1885, the building was purchased by a gentleman named Alfred Blackwater. The house would go on to stay in the ownership of the Blackwater family close to a hundred years, even if it wasn't always lived in. Their ownership culminated in the infamous event of 1982.

7

THE BLACKWATER FAMILY

The purchase of the house by Alfred Blackwater was barely news in the area, which always struck me as odd, considering its well-documented past. But the sale appeared to be a mere footnote, from what I could find.

What is even stranger is that Alfred Blackwater had more than a passing interest in the darker things in life.

Much of Alfred's wealth had been accrued from the trading of artefacts, artwork, and items of historical significance. He had even sold to the Royal Armouries Museum at the Tower of London. But it appeared that while he was a successful trader in his own right, the real reason Alfred pursued this kind of career was to collect items that held a more *personal* interest. His collection of treasures was to be stored at his new home, Perron Manor. I can only assume the place drew his attention precisely because of its notable and disturbing history. Indeed, it is too much of a coincidence to overlook that a man who took such an interest in such things as historic human sacrifice, the release of demons through trepanation, the history of Mesopotamia, and artefacts of demonic entities could buy a place like Perron Manor and not be fully aware of its past.

After taking up residence at the Manor, Alfred Blackwater married a local girl and fathered two boys, the eldest being Timothy Blackwater. When he reached adulthood, Timothy did not see eye-to-eye with his father, and he turned his back on the family home. His younger brother had died at the age of eight, and it is said Timothy had always held Alfred accountable for the death.

During the final years of his life, Alfred remained at Perron Manor alone, having outlived his wife. Not long before his death, one of the darkest and most sickening incidents at Perron Manor (that we know of) took place.

In 1921, Alfred Blackwater commissioned a new heating system for the house. The state-of-the-art, coal-fired furnace would use steam to heat the rest of the house via a piping network fed into large, cast-iron radiators.

Given the size of the property, the installation took a good few weeks. In one of the final days of construction, the youngest worker—a lad named Peter Garrick—was left alone down in the basement with the new furnace. The rest of the workers were on the various floors above, making sure all the pipework and radiators were correctly installed prior to testing. Those on the ground floor heard horrific screaming that was loud and frantic. They also heard the crackle of fire, and the smell of burned meat—which was confusing, given the furnace was not yet lit. However, the first ones to arrive were treated to a horrifying and sickening sight.

Young Peter was trapped in the furnace, stuffed inside the opening, and the flames were devouring him. The door was closed, and the men could see him through the grated opening, and saw his blackened body burn as the young man cried in agony. One man even swore he watched parts of the boy's body burst open, and the very blood was pulled up into the piping system along with the steam and smoke. A horrible hissing sound mixed in with Peter's pained screeching. I am not certain if that is even possible, as I doubt blood could flow upward like that, but the man apparently swore under oath that he was telling the truth. Perhaps it was a delusion from seeing something so horrible, or perhaps it was something else at work?

The men were eventually able to put out the roaring fire within the furnace, but found little left of Peter save for a charred and melted black mess that vaguely resembled a human form.

I find it difficult to put this event down to some unfortunate accident, since the furnace shouldn't have been lit in the first place. Unless Peter was responsible for setting it ablaze, then climbing in to commit suicide in the most horrific of ways, I am forced to assume some other force was at work here.

This is a particularly well-known incident at the house, and local legend says that boy's screams can still be heard when the heating system is started up.

Alfred Blackwater passed away not long after, in 1923. Even though he had not spoken to his only surviving son for many years, the house was willed to the heir, though Timothy refused to live there. He kept the house in his possession, but left it empty.

It wasn't until Timothy died in 1978 and the house was bequeathed to his only child and son—one Marcus Blackwater—that the house was lived in again. Marcus, it seemed, was very much cut from the same cloth as his grandfather, and inheriting Perron Manor was not the burden it had been to his father. However, before we get to that, I feel this is the perfect time to bring the first section of this book to a close. Now, we move on to the more recent past of Perron Manor, one that starts with its vacancy.

Even though the house was empty, it did not stop things from happening. Perron Manor seemed to draw the unsuspecting to it, and we have some of their stories to tell, before we finally get to Marcus and what happened in 1982.

SECTION 2

The Recent History

8

NORMAN CHELMSWICK

Timothy Blackwater despised his father, which is likely one of the reasons he left Perron Manor behind. However, it is also rumoured that, as a boy, he had some quite 'disturbing' experiences there.

It is telling, however, that Timothy did not sell the house, and instead kept it within his ownership. The man was certainly not poor, benefiting from his late father's wealth, but even so, selling a building like the Manor would have no doubt brought in a pretty penny.

And though the house would remain unoccupied until 1978, that doesn't mean it was inactive. Indeed, an abandoned home with a notorious history can prove an alluring place for the bored, curious, or the brave.

The years that passed until Marcus moved in actually prove to be an interesting time. The first incident we will look at took place in the year 1936, covered in a report from the local newspaper, *The Northern Echo*.

It is the story of Norman Chelmswick, and the following is a transcript of that story.

∼

18 June 1936 Edition of *The Northern Echo*.
Vagrant Arrested in Murder House:
The mystery of the missing Alnmouth children was solved yesterday, but be forewarned, the truth behind these disappearances are considered disturbing.

Acting on reports from concerned townsfolk, police from Northumberland Constabulary investigated the long-abandoned Perron Manor, just outside of the town of Alnmouth. There, they found the desecrated bodies of the missing, along with the person responsible for their deaths, one Norman Chelmswick.

The vagrant, a well-known drunkard, seemed to have made the abandoned property his home, but upon entry, police quickly found the man hiding down in the cellar, dressed in a tattered old suit, babbling about the house and what it had made him do.

When questioned, Chelmswick confessed to the murders, saying the house had 'made' him go out into the night and bring back young souls for it to 'feast on,' though he claims he only did it out of fear for his own life, and recited nursery rhymes to the young before he killed them in an effort to soothe their fears.

Six children have gone missing over recent months, and their bodies were all accounted for within the notorious property.

Chelmswick will be charged and put on trial in the coming months. There is little doubt a jury will find him rightfully guilty.

∼

Researching this story a little more, I have found that the missing six consisted of two little girls, and four young boys. Norman Chelmswick was indeed found guilty, and he was sentenced to death by hanging, with the execution taking place in the winter of that same year. Chelmswick, it is claimed, welcomed his death, hoping it would 'quiet the terrible voices in my head.'

9

THE THOMAS SMITH INCIDENT

IN THE YEAR 1955, Perron Manor hit the local headlines again after a young boy—Thomas Smith—went missing. This is something of a pattern with Perron Manor, as you will have no doubt noted.

Thomas Smith's friend, Archie Reynolds, was with him on the evening of the twenty-seventh of October 1955, and they did what two bored young boys are wont to do: get into mischief. With Halloween coming up, what could be better than sneaking into the abandoned house in town that was said to be haunted?

The two of them managed to get inside that night. Archie got back out. Thomas never did.

Back in those days, the incident was a big story in the surrounding area, and the news broke after Archie went to the police (with his parents) and gave his account of what happened, begging the police to go back to the house to save Thomas from 'the things inside.'

Despite the police searching the property extensively, however, Thomas was never found. Archie himself was questioned, but never once changed his story. The case remains officially unsolved, even to this day. But the account Archie gave helped cement the legacy of Perron Manor, despite none of it being verified.

This is an incident I have looked into quite a bit, and I'd planned to go into great detail about myself as part of this book. However, I managed to score something I consider a bit of a 'scoop.' I tracked down Archie Reynolds, and got him to agree—rather reluctantly—to an interview.

It had occurred to me a few years ago that the boy who had been with Thomas Smith the night he disappeared might still be alive, and I knew that a conversation with him would be interesting indeed. However, it was not until I started this book that I began to search for him in earnest. After a few months of sleuthing, I was able to track Archie down, and it turned out that he had moved out of the area to a small town about two hours' drive away. What's more, I was also able to find out his email address.

I contacted Archie and politely requested an interview, explaining who I was and why I wanted to talk. Archie promptly replied and told me to forget it and leave him alone.

Not willing to accept defeat just yet, though, I kept on and asked if it would be possible to speak via a phone call. Eventually, he relented. It was during that call I was able to talk the man round, explaining I would be able to present his side of the story—one often derided by the folks of Alnmouth. And I also told him that, given my experiences, I would certainly believe whatever he told me. Or, at least, I wouldn't dismiss it out of hand, as so many others had done.

So, we arranged for the interview to take place on March 3rd, 2018. I drove to his home, a small bungalow, and recorded the full conversation in audio. What you will read in the next chapter is a full transcript of that interview.

Inside:

Whether you believe what Archie is saying or not, I leave up to you. But I will say this: the man seemed earnest and genuine, in my opinion, even upset and disturbed by what had happened over sixty years ago. Clearly, that night left a very deep emotional scar in the psyche of Archie Reynolds, and it is something I do not believe he has ever truly recovered from.

10

INTERVIEW WITH ARCHIE REYNOLDS, PART 1

ALLOW me to set the scene before we dive into the transcript. Archie was about five-foot-seven, and a little frail, looking every bit his seventy-four years of age. His white hair was thin and frayed, and his hands—gnarled and veiny—tremored involuntarily in his lap, indicating a possible onset of Parkinsons's Disease. The living room of Archie's bungalow felt a little cramped, with cabinets, side tables, an old-fashioned television, a bookcase, and even a piano squeezed into the small space. The walls, too, were littered with framed photographs and artwork of flowers. I immediately noticed many of the pictures were of Archie and a lady with a big, bright smile. He told me it was Agatha, his wife, who had passed three years earlier. I gave him my condolences. Archie said not to worry, that they would meet again in the next life. I asked him how he could be sure of that, how he could truly know there was such a thing as the next life.

'It's the reason you're here, ain't it?' he replied, leveling me with a serious gaze. 'I've known ever since that night. I also know that sometimes the next life isn't necessarily Heaven. It can be a bloody and terrifying Hell.'

And with that, we got down to business.

~

Transcript from the audio tape of Archie Reynolds' interview dated March 3, 2018.

David: Recording. This is David Ritter, paranormal investigator, and I am talking to Archie Reynolds about the incident that took place on the night of October 27, 1955. Archie, can you just confirm for the tape that you were with Thomas Smith that night?

<Pause>

Archie: You know I was. I told you that. That's the whole bloody point of you being here, isn't it?

David: Yes, but as I explained, we may need to go over a few things again, if that's okay? Just for the tape.

<Pause>

Archie: Fine. Yes, I was with Tommy that night.

David: And 'Tommy' is Thomas Smith?

Archie: Aye. But I always knew him as Tommy.

David: And you claim you were both inside Perron Manor the night he went missing?

Archie: You know I was.

David: Yes, but again, it's just for the—

Archie: The tape. Right. Yes, I was with Tommy, and we were inside that bloody house. Never should have been there, though. Single biggest regret of my life, agreeing to go with him.

David: Can you tell me what brought you to Perron Manor that night?

Archie: Stupidity. Stupidity masked with bravado.

David: So, what, was it some kind of dare?

Archie: Not really, we was just bored. Tommy suggested we go up to the old Perron place. It was nearly Halloween, and we'd all heard the stories—

David: Stories?

Archie: About the house. Many people reckoned it was haunted. Lots of whispers about that place between adults, and there were a few local legends that all revolved around that place. Well, to two bored thirteen-year-olds that close to Halloween, how could it not be enticing? Tommy suggested we go up there and see for ourselves what all the fuss was about. I wasn't so sure, knowing that if someone caught us we'd be in a lot of trouble. Tommy was less worried. He said if the place was empty, who would catch us up there? Other lads at school had bragged about finding a way in and walking around the place. I think Tommy was keen to earn some bragging rights of his own. I took a bit of persuading, but in truth it's not like he had to march me up there or anything.

David: So was it already dark by the time you got there?

Archie: Pretty much. Maybe not fully dark, but not far off. I remember standing outside the gate, looking in. Place gave me the creeps right away. First time I'd ever seen it that close. Tommy thought the same. I had no idea how we were going to get in, since the perimeter wall was pretty high, but Tommy had an idea. Said he'd been talking to one of the other boys that had gotten inside. Apparently, if you followed the wall around to the left and reached the side of the property, there were some trees fairly close to the wall. Easy enough to climb up, and close enough to jump onto the top of the wall.

David: So by that logic, you think that your other friends *had* gotten inside, just like they said?

Archie: I guess so.

David: Okay.

<Pause>

Archie: What is it?

David: I'm sorry?

Archie: You gave me a look. Something wrong with what I've just said?

David: No, not at all. I—

Archie: You're thinking, *if those other boys got inside, how come nothing ever happened to them?* Am I right?

David: That's not—

Archie: Well, I don't have an answer for that. But I'll be honest, I wish to God something *had* happened to them. That way me and Tommy would have just stayed the hell away. I spoke to the lads following that night, of course, and asked them about it. They said they heard some weird stuff that freaked them out, but that was it. Apparently they weren't inside for long and ran out after hearing... whatever it was. But, I'll tell you this, most people think I lied about that night. They reckon I had something to do with Tommy's disappearance, in fact. They figure we suffered a misadventure of some kind so I used this story as a cover 'cos I didn't want to come clean. But those boys who had been inside, I could tell they believed me. So no, Mr. Ritter, I don't know why those young lads got away and Tommy didn't. But that's just how it is.

David: Archie, I'm sorry. Really, I am. I didn't mean any disrespect or anything. And I do believe you. But I had to ask about their experience as well, since I'm trying to be thorough.

<Pause>

Archie: Fair enough, I guess. I just don't like when people look at me like I'm crazy.

David: I don't think that, Archie, I promise you. So, you and Tommy climbed the tree and hopped over the wall?

Archie: We did. Nearly shit our pants when we touched down on the other side, too, since we realised we were stuck. Took one look at the wall again and saw there was no way back over. It was too high, and we had nothing to climb on that side.

David: Must have been a little scary.

Archie: More than a little—for me, anyway. Tommy tried to play it cool, said we'd find our way out later.

David: And what did you do from there?

Archie: We walked up to the building and around to the front door. It was locked, of course. At the time, I was relieved. Thought that might be the end of it. We'd shown how brave we were, so if we couldn't go any farther, why not go back? Tommy wasn't convinced. He wanted to keep looking, so we circled round to the back, trudging across the grass as the last of the dusk sky gave way to darkness. I spotted it straight away after we turned the corner to the rear of the house. My heart sank, and I prayed Tommy wouldn't spot it, but... no such luck. Not far from where we stood was a door. A big, thick, wooden one. And it was open.

David: Okay... that's a little strange.

Archie: Indeed. It was swung inwards, showing the darkness inside. I swear, it was like that house was inviting us in. Even Tommy was a little on edge about it, though he still wanted to go in.

David: Did it strike you as odd that a door was just standing open like that?

Archie: Course it did. The other lads who had been inside never mentioned anything about an open door. They told me they got in by jimmying a window. But there it was, wide open. Easy access.

David: And then you went inside?

<Pause>

Archie: Yes. And then we went inside. The place looked kind of how I imagined, to be honest. Lots of dust, and it was run down, but still grand. Stone floors. Ornate frames around the strong oak doors. But it was dark. And it only dawned on us then that we should have brought some kind of torch or something. But we had nothing, so we had to rely on whatever moonlight crept in through the windows. I was fucking terrified at that point, I don't mind telling you. I said to Tommy that we were staying for ten minutes, tops, then I was leaving—without him if I had to.

David: Did he agree to that?

Archie: Yes, he agreed. Didn't do any good, though. That house wasn't about to let us go.

<Pause>

(Note from Author: Archie took a moment here, and I noticed at the time he looked extremely sad. It took him a few seconds to compose himself and push on.)

Archie: I'm okay. I'm actually just a little nervous about talking this through. I live with it every day, and the memory keeps visiting most nights when I'm dreaming. But I've not spoken about it in years. It's harder than I thought it would be.

David: It's okay. In your own time, Archie.

<Pause>

Archie: So, we set off looking around. You know, poking our heads into some of the rooms. Even though we tried to be quiet, it seemed like everything we did caused a loud echo to reverberate off the walls. Ever heard the phrase, 'the silence was deafening?' It was kind of like that. Though 'maddening' might have been a better word choice. The silence seemed to make everything scarier, like the house was just waiting with bated breath. Getting ready to act. We looked into a couple of rooms, and while in one we heard a slam. Loud and quick, like a door had suddenly been forced shut. I jumped out of my skin. Tommy did too. We quickly realised that it had come from the hallway outside. So, we ran out to the hall and saw the external door we had initially come in through was now shut.

David: It might be a stupid question, but is it possible the wind could have caused the door to shut?

Archie: No, not at all. From what I recall, it was a peaceful night—no real wind to speak of. But that wasn't the strangest thing. I ran over to the door, deciding I'd had my fill, and tried to force it open. The fucking thing wouldn't budge.

David: Somehow locked?

Archie: I don't see how it could've been. But it was more than that. The door didn't even rattle in its hinges when I pushed and pulled on it. The damn thing was just stuck fast, impossible to budge, even slightly. Like it was kind of, I dunno, frozen in time or something. I know how that sounds... but it's the truth.

David: So what did you do?

Archie: Other than panic? Well, we stared at each other for a little while, a bit dumfounded. I remember Tommy's eyes at that moment. Wide and full of fear. I knew mine were the same. That was the moment right there, I think, that we both realised something was very wrong with the house. We didn't need to say anything else, and kind of subconsciously agreed on a plan. We ran like hell, sprinting along the corridor, hoping to find another door we could use to get out. We didn't scream, but I could hear our own frantic breathing while we ran. I was struggling to keep it together, coming close to breaking down completely. I kept thinking to myself, *'Just keep going. Push on. You'll get out. And you can figure out what happened tomorrow in the safety of daylight.'* We ran through this big hall, then into another corridor, and our breathing got shorter, more ragged. We weren't tired. It was just the fear, see?

David: I can imagine.

Archie: I'm not sure you can, actually. Not sure you ever want to. We ended up at the main entrance area. There was a big staircase there that went up to the storey above. The double-door to the outside was a big, heavy-looking thing. I knew before we tried it that we'd have no luck. I was right—couldn't open it. Unlike the back one, though, this one rattled in its hinges. Didn't seem to be stuck with the same force, or whatever it was, that had been holding the rear door shut. But it *was* locked, no doubt about that. And we damn sure didn't have the key.

<Pause>

David: Then what happened?

Archie: Then everything went to hell.

11

INTERVIEW WITH ARCHIE REYNOLDS, PART 2

THOUGH THE CONVERSATION CONTINUED UNINTERRUPTED, I felt Archie's last statement was a good place to finish that particular chapter. We will pick up again soon, but I want you to be aware of something. If Archie is to be believed, you are going to read about the final moments of a thirteen-year-old boy. Though the police searched Perron Manor extensively following Thomas' disappearance, he was never found, alive or dead. And the official line has always been that, in all likelihood, Archie and Thomas were not even at Perron Manor on the night of October 27, 1955.

Archie Reynolds claimed differently:

∽

Archie: Tommy let out a little sort of mewl, or cry, when we couldn't get out through the main door. I'll always remember that. Then I remember turning around to look up the stairs. I don't know, I just had a feeling we were being watched, or something. I looked up the flight of stairs leading away from me, then up to the left where one side of the steps branched off to the side, leading to a walkway on the floor above us that doubled back on itself. That's where I saw...

<Pause>

David: What did you see, Archie?

Archie: A person. A man. Whoever it was, he was looking down over the bannister at us. At Tommy, specifically. The man's face... Jesus, I can never forget that. Pale as the moon, and eyes that were just black pits. I let out a scream, and then the man just pulled back out of view. Tommy panicked, asking what I had seen, but I couldn't bring myself to speak, I just kept stuttering. Then we heard footsteps. Heavy, thudding footsteps on the walkway above us, moving along towards the stairs. And just as it sounded like this person should have come into our view, the footsteps stopped. And there was nothing.

David: He stopped?

Archie: He just wasn't there anymore. We waited for a few moments, scared out of our wits, but knew we couldn't just stay like that forever. Eventually, we picked up enough courage to edge forward and look up the stairs. We saw the walkway above, pretty much in full view now, but there was no one there.

David: And, to be clear, you believe the person you saw was a... ghost?

Archie: I know it was. Knew it straight away at the time —as soon as I looked into the gaping black holes where his eyes should have been.

David: And then what happened?

Archie: Well, we ran again—what else could we do? Did a full loop of the goddamn building and ended up where we started, at that back door, which was still stuck. We weren't getting out. Tommy had the bright idea to smash one of the windows. There were a few that looked out to a courtyard from the corridor we were in. Neither of us wanted to break through glass with our bare hands—there wasn't such a thing as safety glass back then, you know—so we ducked into one of the rooms to find something to use. First room we come to, we find this big, metal candlestick holder. A heavy thing, free-standing, about as tall as we were. Tommy hoisted it up, and we marched back out of the room, right to a window—there was someone standing directly outside. A horrible-looking, rotting woman. Skin was dark and mottled. I could see bone through her cheeks. No lips. Just teeth and black gums. No eyes, either. She just stood there, outside, in a dirty, torn, white dress. She was totally still as well. And I don't just mean she stood still, I mean there was no movement at all. Like she was... was...

David: Frozen in time?

Archie: Exactly! We screamed, of course. Tommy dropped the candlestick and we ran yet again. But my legs were like jelly. I knew we could run and run, but we'd only ever go round in circles until we couldn't run anymore. As it was, we had to stop, and we ended up in that big hall again. It was a huge room. And, up ahead, we spotted another figure, standing in front of a door. Again, it didn't move, but this one was tall—unnaturally so, with long arms. I couldn't make out much more as the thing was mostly hidden in shadows. It just stood there, blocking the way. Then we heard a laughing sound behind us. A horrible fucking noise, like the cackling of a witch, getting closer. And we could also hear quick, approaching footsteps, like someone was running towards us. There was a door off to our side, so we dashed through and came to a set of stone steps that led downward. It was dark, but what other choice did we have? I didn't think it at the time, but in retrospect I realise we were being funnelled down there. And we went. Couldn't see a damn thing.

David: I remember this from one of the news reports I found regarding the incident. It claimed that you said you were both forced down to the basement where 'something happened,' and that's where you lost Thomas.

Archie: I said a lot more than that, I can tell you.

David: So, what exactly happened down there?

Archie: It was pitch black. We ended up falling down the steps, since we couldn't see a damn thing. I hurt my ankle, and ended up landing on top of Tommy. I heard him wheezing. We just kind of laid there for a moment in fright, almost sobbing. I honestly thought I was going to die. I whispered to Tommy that we had to move. Didn't want to raise my voice in case there was something down there that could hear us. There *was* something there, of course. From the dark, we heard a dry and pained moan. Just about pissed myself, I did. Then, I felt something, seemed like a sudden blast of cold near us. I told Tommy that we needed to move. Shouted it. Then we heard a voice just above us. It said Tommy's name, but drew the word out. '*Toooommyyyyy.*' That fucking voice. It sounded dead. Devoid of anything human. Absolutely fucking evil. Then it said, '*Come with us.*' We were both crying now, not able to hide it or keep quiet.

<*Author Note: Archie stayed silent for a few moments and had tears in his eyes. He looked extremely pale.*>

David: Take your time.

Archie: I felt it... I felt that fucking thing touch me.

<*Author Note: Archie quietly sobbed a little here, and had tears running down his face.*>

Archie: It... it grabbed my wrist. I remember how tight that grip was. And how cold it was. I felt my skin actually sting. I cried out, but then felt myself be thrown back. I panicked and flailed around, and then I heard Tommy scream. He kept shouting my name, begging me to help him. There was a scraping sound, and his cries started to move away from me. Something was dragging him deeper into the darkness. I feel ashamed now, of course, but all I could think about at the time was getting the hell out of there. As I flailed around, my hand hit something hard. It was the bottom stone step. I remember that I paused for a moment, listening to Tommy scream for me. But I was just too scared. When I heard another horrible, cold laugh come from the dark where Tommy was, that was it... I... I just scrambled up the stairs. Came out at the top and ran, not looking anywhere but straight ahead. Felt like my legs were going to give out, but I forced myself forward. Reached the back door again and—I promise you, I'm not lying here—the thing was open. Wide open. Ready for me to run through.

David: But you'd tried that door before, right?

Archie: Yes. It had been stuck shut then, but not now. So I ran out into the night. Sprinted to the wall and tried to climb over. Took me a few attempts, but I just dug my fingers into the mortar joints hard enough to cut my fingers and rip off a few nails. Didn't feel it at the time, though. Not until I was halfway home, when I managed to calm myself down enough to feel anything but fear. The adrenaline wore off, see. Then I just dropped to the street and cried. Don't remember a lot, other than seeing a hand-mark on my wrist. It was bright red, where that thing had grabbed me. Apparently, a passerby found me and stopped to help. Claims they couldn't get much sense out of me beyond jabbering hysterically about the old Perron House, and how it had my friend. I managed to sputter out my address, and they took me home. I told my parents everything. They didn't believe much of it, of course, but were worried enough about Tommy to get the police involved. And then the circus started. The police say they searched the house, but found nothing. No sign of either him or anyone else.

David: And they searched the basement?

Archie: So they said, yes. No one believed me, but a few of the local papers got wind that Tommy was missing—and they also heard what I'd told the police. Didn't take the stories long to appear in the rags after that. Headlines like, 'Boy claims friend taken by Spook House,' and the like. Some tried to interview me, but my parents wouldn't have it.

David: Can you tell me anything about the investigation that followed? The search for Thomas?

Archie: Not much. I didn't have a lot of involvement. The police questioned me a few times, and I think they were under the impression I was lying. One even told me as much, and he was annoyed that I didn't once change my tune. He seemed to think I was covering something up, and that we'd more than likely gone somewhere we weren't supposed to—his guess was the quarry outside of town—and then Tommy had had an accident which resulted in his death. But there was no evidence, no body, no nothing. So, nothing came of it. And Tommy's mam and dad had to live with that, never really knowing, because I can tell you they weren't prepared to believe what I'd told everyone. Weren't willing to accept the truth. Can't say I blame them, of course. If it hadn't happened to me, I wouldn't have believed it either.

David: It must have been tough for you.

Archie: That's an understatement. My family and I didn't stick around in town long after that. We moved away, and I've never been back since.

David: Can't say I blame you. I have to ask, though... why do you think that door was open when you got out, given it had been held shut before?

Archie: Damned if I know. If I were to guess, though, I'd say the house let me go. Didn't want me—it wanted Tommy. I was inconsequential. No idea why, and to be honest, I try not to think about that too much. Don't want to pull at that thread, you know what I mean?

David: I guess so.

Archie: Now let me ask *you* something. Why the interest in that place?

David: Perron Manor?

Archie: Yes. Why are you so obsessed with it?

David: Well, I'm not sure 'obsessed' is the right word. But I will admit to having a strong interest in the house.

Archie: Why? You obviously know what happened there in the eighties.

David: Of course. You know about that?

Archie: I do. Obviously, given what happened to me, I believe the truth has a certain *paranormal* element to it.

David: Me too, and that's why I'm drawn to it. I honestly believe there is something there. Something beyond what we can understand. And that is *very* interesting to me.

Archie: Yeah, but... that house is evil. You understand that, right? It isn't a place that should be studied. It should be knocked down. If you knew the truth about that place, why the hell did you go in looking for this kind of stuff?

David: Erm... you know about my investigation?

Archie: Well, when I agreed to this interview, I did some

research of my own. Wanted to know who I was dealing with. I was happy enough you would believe me, which was comforting. I know you'll let me get my side of the story out there. At the same time, I was a little troubled as to why someone would *want* to go there, if they believed the truth about Perron Manor—as you clearly do.

David: Isn't it obvious? It's proof of life after death. That there is more to our existence than we know. Why wouldn't I want to know as much about it as I could?

Archie: As it happens, that was the other reason I was keen to meet. I wanted to see if I couldn't talk some sense into you. The thing is, life after death isn't necessarily a good thing. Certainly not for the souls trapped in that house. I firmly believe they are doomed to suffer there forever. That's why you should think very long and very hard about ever going back. Otherwise, you could find out just how much of a Hell life after death can be.

David: Well, I don't know that I share your view, but it doesn't matter anyway. The owner has made it clear he doesn't want us back. Ever.

Archie: And yet you're itching to return. I can tell. Keep away, my boy. Let the place rot.

<End of interview.>

~

It was at this point I stopped the tape. We talked a little more, but just covered old ground—there was nothing in that discussion that warrants inclusion here. However, the interview itself is fascinating to me. The sceptic would discount everything he said as fantasy, of course, but I can tell you this: whether it happened or not, Archie Reynolds certainly believed what he was telling me. So, he either imagined the whole thing and has gone through life thinking it is real, or everything he described *did* in fact happen. While my opinion on the matter is no doubt obvious, I'll leave you to make up your own minds on what really took place that night.

12

THE INTERVENING YEARS

THE STORIES SURROUNDING the building grew the longer the house stood empty. Locals had always been wary of the place, but since the disappearance of Thomas Smith, that suspicion and mistrust only increased. I have interviewed scores of people who had stories about 'old Perron Manor,' and all of them were fascinating.

Indeed, one only needs to venture into one of the local drinking establishments in Alnmouth and begin speaking to some of the more elderly locals to hear stories of your own.

Some of the tales I've been told include:

A man who claimed that, as teenagers, he and his friends used to go up to the grounds of the abandoned house at night to drink and smoke and get up to the kind of trouble kids tend to. That all stopped, however, one particular night. They noticed that one of the ground-floor windows was ajar, and decided to sneak inside. The man who told me this story, and another of the group, started to climb inside, but quickly froze when they saw someone standing on the other side of the room. The man claims that a shadowy figure was there, 'hidden by robes,' and 'stood as still as a photo.' It was only when the figure raised its head, so that the two young men could see the face beneath, that the pair escaped and 'ran for their lives.' The man claimed the face he saw, twisted and decayed, still gives him nightmares to this day.

A woman accompanied her father up to the house one day, when she was young. The father was a local plumber, and the owner of the house—who she stated didn't live there at the time—employed her dad to go to the house one Saturday to fix a leaking water pipe. The father had been on babysitting duty, so figured he could just take his daughter with him, as it was supposed to be a quick fix. The woman remembered getting up to the house with her dad and found the front door unlocked, as the owner had said it would be. They entered, and her father got to work. At one point, he had to go down to the cellar, so he told his daughter to wait at the top of the stairs for him. She recalled how, after he disappeared into the darkness with his torch guiding the way, she heard only silence for a few moments, then the sudden sound of her father gasping in fright. 'What the fuck *are* you?' she heard him say. Then, there was a deep, sinister cackle, followed by an ungodly shriek. Her father came bounding back up the steps, white as a sheet, grabbed her, and they sprinted out of the house. As they ran, her father demanded the girl not look back. He never finished the job, refused payment, and flatly refused to ever go back to that place again.

Lastly, I once spoke with two brothers who, when in their early twenties, went up to Perron Manor at night. They'd heard the stories and wanted to see it for themselves, since they'd just moved into the area. The two didn't even make it inside, however. They chose a window to try and get in through, given the doors seemed locked, but after they approached it and pushed at the frame, one of them looked up to see someone standing on the other side of the glass, staring out at them. This strange person had not been there while the brothers had approached, and yet now gazed back at them with 'dead eyes,' only a few inches away. It was a woman, they claimed, and her skin was withered, with lidless eyes bulging out of her head. The pair didn't stick around and ran.

These are only a few of the stories I've heard that supposedly took place between the years 1923 and 1978, and although they are only hearsay, and not provable, they are still of great interest and relevance. In my view, they go a long way in proving that, even when abandoned, the house is never *truly* empty.

As previously noted, in 1978, the owner of Perron Manor —Timothy Blackwater—passed away. The property was then transferred into the ownership of his only son, Marcus.

13

MARCUS BLACKWATER

Unlike his father, who wanted nothing to do with Perron Manor, Marcus Blackwater had a very strong interest in the property he had inherited. His interests aligned much more with those of his grandfather, and Marcus was a keen student of all things occult. To come into possession of a house such as Perron Manor, given the history that went with it, must have been a dream come true.

Marcus moved into the house immediately. As an added bonus, he now also possessed the artefacts that his grandfather had left behind as well. Marcus soon began studying what had been handed down to him.

He also allowed a friend to live in the house with him, an old acquaintance from his university days who had remained close. This man also had a love for the occult, so Marcus saw him as a perfect person to share the large space with. This man was Vincent Bell.

Vincent is someone with whom I have spoken, and it was he, more than anyone, who revealed to me what actually happened on the night of Halloween 1982. On top of that, he also conveyed the type of person Mr. Blackwater really was. Marcus was charming, handsome, and pleasant, and he had a gift for putting people at ease. But beneath that warm exterior—Vincent claimed—Marcus was driven and single-focused, truly caring only about himself and his goals. Vincent lamented to me that he found out who the real Marcus Blackwater was all too late, and that he feels a sense of responsibility for what happened back then, though he can scarcely explain the events.

And that is the real issue with that night in 1982. *No one can really explain it.* However, I will present you the facts as I know them, which are taken from news reports at the time, eyewitness accounts, and a testimony from Vincent Bell that occurred when I investigated Perron Manor in 2013.

For reasons unclear at the time, it seemed Marcus Blackwater had plans for the home he inherited. Not satisfied with simply coming into the ownership of a magnificent building, and the many strange and interesting artefacts within, Marcus also wanted to turn the large property into a functioning hotel.

Vincent recalls that the idea perplexed him, and it seemed to come out of nowhere, but Marcus was adamant. So, they got to work. It was at this time Vincent told his friend that he had a sister who had worked in the hospitality sector and had previous experience in hotels. What's more, her husband was also an accomplished handyman. Vincent asked if the two would be interested in working for him, for a good salary. As it turned out, they very much were, and they agreed to join.

Vincent's sister, Rita, and her husband, Ray, moved into Perron Manor, with their young daughter, Chloe. Though other contractors came and went, the core five remained, working on the house and getting it ready for a new life as a hotel, which went on to open in March, 1982.

Inside:

The Blackwater Hotel.

Business was steady, it seemed, with a trickle of guests passing through. The problem, Vincent's sister said, was the location. Though it was a wonderful setting, the town of Alnmouth was not the kind of place many people visited. Marcus, however, did not seem perturbed, and he appeared happy enough with the amount of patronage they received. At least for the time being. Soon, he revealed a plan to boost the profile of the establishment: he wanted to hold an event. He said every room in the hotel would be rented out free of charge for one weekend, and dignitaries and well-known socialites from the local area would be invited for a relaxing getaway. Though it would be a financial burden, Marcus seemed confident that the press and buzz the free weekend would generate would be more than worth it. So, a plan was put into place, and arrangements were made. There was plenty of interest, and that weekend the hotel was booked out close to capacity.

And the pièce de résistance? Marcus had decided that, due to the notorious history of Perron Manor, an ideal theme for the event would be to make it a haunted weekend, where guests would learn about some of the terrible things that had happened in the past; he told them they might even see ghosts themselves. Finally, Marcus arranged the event to fall on Halloween.

14

GAINING MOMENTUM

THE FOLLOWING IS from a newspaper article that appeared in *The Northern Echo* newspaper on the run-up to the event.

∽

29 September 1982 Edition of *The Northern Echo*.
Halloween Haunting at New Hotel:
The old Perron Manor is a name that may be unknown to many, but to the locals of Alnmouth, it is one that will likely evoke at least some recognition, if not strong feelings of dread. There are multitudes of stories and legends that surround that old house, which isn't surprising given its storied history.

And it appears the current owner—Marcus Blackwater, who turned the house into a hotel earlier this year—is well aware of that. In fact, it seems he is using it to his advantage.

In what seems like a carefully crafted marketing plan, Mr. Blackwater has announced that every room in the hotel over Halloween weekend will be rented out for free, to chosen applicants. The owner of the Blackwater Hotel has stated that guests will enjoy an event-packed time where they can learn of the history of the building, take a full tour of the premises, and even partake in ghost hunting themselves, before sleeping in one of the many supposedly haunted rooms.

While this reporter seriously doubts any headless apparitions will appear, it is hard not to appreciate the effort and ingenuity that has gone into boosting the hotel's profile.

The hotel manager, Mrs. Rita Pearson, confirmed there are still some spaces available, and anyone interested should contact the hotel directly to apply.

15

THE GATHERING

As THE BIG day grew closer, the buzz surrounding the event reached an impressive level, especially for a hotel as relatively unknown as the Blackwater. Whoever was in charge of the public relations push (I have a feeling it was Rita Pearson, the manager) had done a good job. Even some of the locals I have spoken to recently remembered people talking about it, even if they all originally thought it was a just hokey publicity stunt.

The event started on the afternoon of Friday the twenty-ninth of October, 1982. Guests arrived and were treated to a welcome speech by Marcus, who went into a little of the house's history.

After this, guests were allowed to settle into their rooms, unpack, and ready themselves for an evening meal that was to be held in the large ground-floor dining hall. Excitement was in the air, and the guests all seemed to be having a good time. A tour of the building followed, and then the dining hall was again opened up as an entertainment area, complete with alcoholic beverages, before everyone retired for the evening.

It wasn't until the next morning, when the guests all met for breakfast, that word began to spread of certain 'happenings' during the night.

Some guests told of hearing strange things, and some swore they even saw people who should not have been there; one woman was certain a man had been standing outside of her ground-floor bedroom window, peering in. Supposedly, that lady left the next day, terrified at what she'd seen, and did not return.

I think it is fair to say that most—if not *all*—of the gathered patrons were not really expecting to see anything supernatural, and had probably been focused on having a fun weekend. However, after that first night, it is said that the mood began to change, with many people wondering: *what if this place really is haunted?*

According to reports, the second day progressed with more occurrences and experiences, all fleeting, but enough that tension and even excitement grew.

While Vincent was initially a fan of what Marcus was trying to do, he explained it was the Saturday when he began to seriously suspect that Marcus had some ulterior motive for the weekend, and that it was building to something that Vincent wanted no part of. Indeed, Vincent claims he even tried to confront Marcus about his worries, but was given no time, with Marcus reacting angrily to anything he said.

And if the previous night had some creepy occurrences, then Saturday night ramped things up, with more sightings and incidents reported to have taken place. Also, three guests were assumed to have fled in the night. However, police would go on to report that those people were never found; whatever happened to them remains a mystery. Panic levels rose and it took a speech from Marcus the following morning at breakfast to settle everyone's nerves, which he managed to do.

And so Sunday, Halloween, continued in a similar vein. But it is the third night that will live in infamy.

16

TRAGEDY STRIKES

THIS ARTICLE APPEARED in *The Northern Echo* two days after Halloween.

∼

02 November 1982 Edition of *The Northern Echo*.
Horror at Blackwater Hotel:

Tragedy struck at Blackwater Hotel on Sunday night, with police still trying to piece together what actually led to multiple deaths and disappearances.

The hotel was host to a well-publicised 'haunted weekend' event, and was close to capacity. Authorities were called to an incident that was occurring at the hotel during the early hours of Monday morning, and when they arrived, they were met with horrific scenes that were more fitting to a movie than to reality.

The initial reports from the townsfolk of Alnmouth were due to hearing strange noises coming from the building. Given the distance to the property from the surrounding town, the fact any sounds were able to travel that far, and even wake people during the night, is quite surprising. Worried residents reported hearing faint screams, and worse, as one person put it, 'a deep, guttural rumbling... never heard anything like it before in my life.'

The state of the deceased is said to have been sickening, with very few bodies actually left whole or intact. Stranger still, considering the number of people who were staying at the hotel that weekend, the number of the dead did not line up, and police currently have no idea what has happened to the missing patrons.

The hotel owner, Mr. Marcus Blackwater, was found dead as well, though it appears he had taken his own life by cutting his throat. His lifeless body was lying in what our source claims to be a strange symbol drawn on the floor in blood. It is also reported that there are only four survivors accounted for.

We await more facts to emerge over this horrific event, but for now, our thoughts are with the missing and the families of the deceased.

17

THAT FATEFUL NIGHT

AS YOU WILL HAVE SEEN from the preceding newspaper article, something terrible took place that night in 1982. Given the small number of survivors, finding out exactly what that was is difficult.

The missing people were never found, and in the following days it was confirmed that the only survivors were a few of the staff from the Blackwater Hotel: Vincent Bell, Rita Pearson, Ray Pearson, and their young child Chloe Pearson.

Obviously, the police pulled all of them in for questioning, to try and piece together what happened. However, they soon determined that all of the survivors appeared to be just as in the dark as the police were, with none of them able to explain what happened, other than giving evidence that was... difficult to believe. They each relayed as much as they knew, but the stories they told were, according to reports, fantastical—though told earnestly, at least in the opinion of the interviewing officers.

Even Vincent, who had an interest in the dark and

occult, distanced himself from the 'mad man' Marcus Blackwater.

There was no evidence to charge any of the survivors, and so, after months and months of investigation and a local media whirlwind, the police dialled back investigations. Within two years, the case was closed and marked as unsolved, which it remains to this day.

Lots of stories circulate about what happened that night, and many locals all have their own theories: a suicide pact carried out by a widespread cult; Marcus Blackwater being a killer who took his own life to avoid being caught; and even supernatural intervention, where the spirits of the house came to feast on the living.

When I was finally able to speak to Vincent Bell in 2013, he gave me a lot of information, but said he was unable to tell me too much about that night, as his mind had blocked out a lot of what had happened. All he remembered was lots of screaming, lots of fear, and watching 'people get pulled into the very walls.'

I knew Vincent was being evasive, and not fully honest, but no amount of pressing could yield any further information. I have been unable to track down the other survivors—Rita, Ray, and their daughter, Chloe—to interview, meaning one of the more famous events to take place at Perron Manor lacks many crucial details.

So, all we know with any certainty is that: many people died, with their bodies torn apart and desecrated; Marcus Blackwater took his own life; a lot of the guests disappeared and were unaccounted for amongst the dead, and they have still not been found to this day. Not a single one.

And lastly, we know that Marcus Blackwater left the property to Vincent Bell in his will.

I asked Vincent why he thought this was, and Vincent

seemed to think it was so someone would be around to keep the legacy of Perron Manor going. However, Vincent claimed he decided to keep the house and stay there, 'so that no one else would have to suffer the darkness the house brought with it.'

Perron Manor, as it once again became known, was understandably given a wide berth by everyone in Alnmouth. Vincent Bell kept to himself, becoming almost a recluse, so there is little else to report regarding the history of what I believe to be the most haunted house in Britain.

Except for one thing: in 1985, a young girl named Katie Evans, a local to Alnmouth, disappeared and was last seen wandering close to the Manor. Despite investigating, police found no trace of her up there.

Now, it may be that her disappearance has nothing to do with the house at all. Or, perhaps it does. Given the history, it would be foolish to rule out the possibility completely.

Being a paranormal researcher, I dearly wanted to investigate Perron Manor, more than any other location I'd heard about. And for many years, that looked like it would be an impossibility.

However, all that changed in 2013.

SECTION 3

The Investigation

18

INVESTIGATION PART 1

As I'm sure you can imagine, Perron Manor played a huge part in developing my interest in the paranormal. Over the years, I tried multiple times to contact the owner—Vincent Bell—with the hope of carrying out an investigation there. This was my 'white whale.' But, despite my best efforts both in writing to and trying to visit Vincent in person, he rebuffed and ignored my requests. I kept up my persistence, but was always met with the same response, so you can imagine my surprise when in 2013, Vincent Bell actually contacted *me*, by letter, telling me he was happy to facilitate an investigation over two pre-specified nights. He left a number, so I called him. Though abrupt during the brief talk, he confirmed he was happy for an investigation to go ahead. I couldn't believe it, nor could I understand why the recluse had so suddenly changed his mind, but I was not about to look this gift horse in the mouth.

My investigation was green-lit!

The rest of my team—which consisted of Jenn Hogan, Ralph Cobin, Jamie Curtis, Ann Tate, and George Dalton—were all as excited as I was, and though it is dangerous to get carried away prior to an investigation lest you lose any semblance of objectivity, I felt confident that the expedition would blow us away.

We had just over two weeks to prepare, which was plenty of time to make any personal arrangements we needed to. During that period, I tried to research the building and grounds in even more detail. I knew quite a lot about Perron Manor already, given my obsession with it, but the upcoming investigation gave me extra impetus to learn everything I could. It was a worthwhile endeavour, as most of the knowledge I crammed into that two-week period formed the basis for this book. It also focused our minds for what to expect going in, and how to structure our expedition.

Like a child anticipating Christmas Day, the wait seemed to last an eternity. Eventually, the big day rolled around, and we all headed over to Perron Manor and loaded into my transit van, which was large enough to hold us all and our equipment.

Vincent Bell met us at the iron entrance gates and opened them up for us without a word, before beckoning us inside. The thin, frail man gave us no smile or warmth, and barely made eye contact. He did speak, however.

'We walk down from here.'

Given the entrance gate opened up to a long gravel driveway which ran down to the building, I asked if we could bring the van down closer to the house in order to make unloading easier. To be honest, I'd asked the question out of courtesy, not for one moment thinking it would be a problem. Our host, though, turned his pale blue eyes to the van, curled his top lip, then shook his head.

'No,' was his single-word reply.

I did not get the chance to change his mind as he turned

Inside:

and started to walk back towards the house. My team and I cast each other confused glances, got out of the van, and followed Vincent down.

'But we need our equipment,' I said. 'Is there any reason why we can't bring then van closer?'

'Yes. Because I said so,' he replied.

His tone was abrasive, and he made no effort to hide the scowl he was wearing. Despite him having agreed to this whole thing in person, I got the distinct impression Vincent *didn't* actually want us there, and having to traipse up and down the long driveway every time we needed something was going to make things more difficult. I knew I had to broach this again, but I fell silent when we reached Perron Manor.

I'd seen the property before, of course, mostly from afar. But being inside of its grounds, looking up at the imposing building before me and knowing that I would spend the next two nights here investigating the paranormal... well, it brought shivers down my spine. An excitable fear is the best way to describe what I felt at that moment. My team felt it, too.

We just knew that this place would deliver for us.

Perron Manor didn't disappoint.

19

INVESTIGATION PART 2

'Would it be possible,' I started, speaking to Vincent, 'if we just brought the van down to the entrance, unloaded everything, then stored the gear inside? We can move the van back outside the gates straight after, if that helps.'

I saw this as a reasonable compromise to his decidedly unreasonable stance. We were walking along a short corridor, and he was giving us a tour of the ground floor as I asked the question. The rest of the team trailed behind.

'You can make do where it is,' he replied. 'Or you can leave.'

I still couldn't make sense of his attitude. After all, Vincent had previously agreed to my proposal of an investigation. In the flesh, though, his attitude was quite different.

'Do you not want us here?' I asked, dreading his response. I desperately didn't want my investigation to fall through, but I knew it just wouldn't work if the owner of the property was going to be this difficult. I've investigated locations in the past when the owners or residents were present and caused problems, and they had only ever ended in failure.

Vincent stopped and turned to face me. His eyes narrowed and he bared his teeth ever so slightly.

'No,' he replied, and I felt my heart drop. For whatever reason, it was clear he'd changed his mind about things. I could feel the opportunity I'd waited for my whole adult life slipping away. But then he turned his head and stared off into the distance of the corridor. It was like he was listening to something, and I noted a distinctly uneasy look on his face. Maybe even fear. Then, he nodded solemnly and turned back to face me.

'You can bring your van and get your stuff," he said. A bony finger was then in my face as Vincent stepped forward. 'But then you move it back. Understand?'

I nodded. 'No problem.'

'Good. Now, I'm sure you don't need me to show you around anymore. You can explore as you need to. Just leave me be and get on with what you need to do. My room is number six, on the floor above us. That is off-limits. I'll see you again in the morning... if you're still here.'

And with that, he was gone.

'He sure changed his tune quickly,' Jenn said. 'I thought he was about to kick us out.'

'Is it just me,' I started to say, 'or did it seem like someone was communicating with him just before he changed his mind?'

'It kind of did,' Ralph agreed. 'He even nodded at something.'

'Did anyone feel a drop in temperature or anything like that?' I asked, my mind immediately springing into action. Had we just witnessed a paranormal interaction, thanks to the owner of the Manor? If we had, a sudden feeling of cold —a marker of a supernatural presence—could help prove it. Sadly, no one had noticed anything, myself included.

Rather than continue the self-guided tour, we decided it best to go back for the van and unload all the equipment while we still had daylight. For now, we could just store it in the entrance foyer, at least until we got set up. On the way back up the driveway, Jenn looked over her shoulder to the house. She stopped and pointed, eyes going wide.

'Top floor, window to the far left!' We all spun around, and I quickly located the window she was pointing to. It looked the same as most of the others: white-painted timber frames with Georgian bars crossing both vertically and horizontally. I could just make out curtains tied back to both sides, but other than that, there was nothing.

'What?' Ralph asked.

'Someone was looking out,' Jenn said. 'Couldn't make out who, but there was *definitely* a figure there.'

'Vincent?' George asked. 'Perhaps that's room six?'

'Could be,' I said. 'Odd numbering if six is all the way up there, though. Jenn, did it look like Vincent?'

'Hard to say,' she responded. 'They stepped out of view almost as soon as I saw them.'

We continued staring up at the window, but whoever it was didn't make a reappearance.

'Let's keep going,' I eventually said, not sure what to make of it. If things were starting to happen already, we needed to get our arses in gear and bring our equipment inside. The entire excursion would be pointless if we failed to get any evidence to back up our experiences. I was determined not to let that happen.

20

INVESTIGATION PART 3

UNLOADING ALL our stuff took a little over half an hour, and when we finished, Ralph brought the van back outside of the entrance gates. It was a pointless gesture, but we did it to appease Vincent. I had a feeling that by being so pedantic, he was trying to show us who was boss. So be it. As long as we could continue, I cared little about one-upmanship. Since Vincent had retired for the evening, we had free rein.

The entrance foyer was grand, but aged. Our shoes clicked and clacked on the stone-tile floor. Corridors and rooms to the left and right of the foyer were accessed by large, oak doors with brass handles. Opposite the entrance door was a flight of wooden stairs that had a runner of red carpet central to the wide steps. The stairs led up to a half-landing, then split off both left and right, with each side going up to the floor above. A large, high window gave a view out to the central courtyard from the half-landing, and that window allowed plenty of natural light to spill into the foyer.

We had littered the floor with our equipment: video cameras, thermal cameras, monitors, various audio recorders, laptops, batteries, bundles and bundles of wires and cabling, food and water supplies, and a plethora of other items we always brought with us. When investigating, it is fair to say that I preferred myself and my team to be overprepared.

However, we couldn't just leave everything on the floor as the foyer looked like a bomb site. I'd found some floor plans of the building online, and knew there was a suitable room accessed directly from the foyer, just off to the left. It was a study of some kind, and it had a sturdy oak table set centrally within it.

'Looks like a perfect HQ,' Jamie said after we investigated. I had to agree.

The study was therefore to be our base of operations. All the equipment was moved into it, and we began setting up in earnest. We had plenty of dust covers with us, so we threw them over the table to ensure nothing scratched the polished surface. Our monitors and laptops were set upon the dining table, with plenty of room to spread everything out.

'Do you think we should take a tour of the place before completing the set-up?' Ralph asked. 'We still have a bit of daylight left.'

It was a good point; however, I was concerned that if we didn't have recording equipment with us, anything that happened during that initial walk around would go undocumented, save for our own testimony. I also had a feeling that things would start happening quickly now that we were here.

Still, we needed to get our bearings, and Ralph was absolutely correct that we should familiarise ourselves with the place while we had natural light to aid us.

For whatever reason—and we can attest to this from our

own previous investigations—paranormal activity always seems to be more prevalent at night. So, we put a pin in our preparations for the time being.

'Everyone make sure you have handheld cameras, though,' I said. 'Ralph, bring something for audio, too. I want to limit the walk around to an hour and a half if we can, so try and take note of your surroundings and memorise as much as possible.'

I also brought along the printouts of the floor plans I had. I had no clue if they were accurate, but at least it was something.

And then we set off to explore Perron Manor in earnest for the first time.

21

INVESTIGATION PART 4

THE WALK around took longer than the planned hour and a half, lasting just over two hours. And that still felt like we were going at a quick pace. In hindsight, I should have expected that. While the building wasn't the largest we had ever investigated (we'd been to museums, hotels, and even a prison), there was just so much to see and get caught up in that it made for slow progress.

We took a logical approach to our exploration, doing a full lap of the ground floor before repeating the process with the floor above, and once more for the top storey. Lastly, we descended all the way back down and moved to the basement level.

The layout was, I found, roughly the same as the floor plans I'd uncovered online. Some rooms had a different use than what was noted on the plans, but overall they were pretty accurate. The ground floor was a mix of living spaces, a dining room, toilets, a large, almost commercial-sized kitchen, and even a great hall. There were also some bedrooms to the rear of the property as well, which makes sense considering its previous use as a hotel. Whether they were always used as bedrooms, however, or had been converted to such, I am not sure. The floor above consisted mainly of bedrooms, two large bathrooms, storage rooms, and so on, with the top storey, set within the roof space, being predominantly bedrooms, though one area was locked and, apparently, out of bounds. The basement level was interesting, especially knowing its history, and one could still discern the layout of what would have been cells and holding areas. Now, however, it was used as a boiler room for the antiquated heating system, and also seemed to be a messy and unkempt storage area.

Despite the walk around taking a while, there were no incidents or occurrences to note, other than all members mentioning the feeling of being watched at some point or another, including myself. But there is no way to prove a feeling, of course, so we could do no more than make a note of it. With the initial exploration out of the way, it was time to finish setting up.

We arranged our laptops, which would show the readings from various other pieces of equipment, on the table in our makeshift HQ. The first hurdle we had to overcome, but one we were prepared for, was the lack of Wi-Fi in the building. It seems inconceivable in today's world to not have an internet connection, but Vincent Bell obviously saw things differently. He had a phone line, and that was about it. Fortunately, we'd known we would have to rely on Bluetooth signals between equipment. The downside to that, however, was that said signal could only reach so far, meaning we would have to be tactical in where we positioned any stationary equipment we had, which would then feed back to the laptops.

For this reason, we positioned a night-vision-compatible camera in the entrance foyer, and then dotted some around the rooms in the vicinity of the dining hall. From HQ, the signal was able to just barely pick up the basement level, or at least part of it, and we had half-decent coverage on the floor above as well. We even managed to have a wall-mounted camera outside, which picked up the courtyard. The top storey of the building proved a bridge too far, however, meaning we would have to cover that area, and many other places, on foot. After all, we only had so many cameras, and in many of the bigger locations we had investigated most of the work was done on handheld equipment anyway.

The handheld cameras used digital videotapes, while the stationary ones relayed everything back to the laptops, which then recorded everything they picked up. It was the same with the audio equipment.

By the time we had finished setting everything up, dusk had set in, so we were just in time.

We monitored the stationary cameras for a little while from HQ while we prepared for the first part of the night's activities. Given there were six of us, we would split up into three two-person teams. One rule I have during any investigation is that we don't do things alone, so each group had a different assignment, for the purpose of drawing out some activity.

Ralph and Jamie would go up to the uppermost floor with sound-recording equipment (as well as their handheld cameras) and try to catch some Electronic Voice Phenomena, by asking questions of any spirits that may have been present. As a group, we were seasoned enough to know that while we may not hear anything at the time of asking, the real test of success would be when we played the recordings back. Often, recording equipment can pick up voices that are not audible to the human ear, possibly coming through in frequencies we are not attuned to. We have captured voice recordings before of things we did not initially hear, where someone—or something—was quite clearly responding to the questions asked of it.

George and Ann were to conduct a séance in the great hall near the back of the property, since Ann has a certain sensitivity to ghosts and spirits. While not quite what I would call a full medium, she is certainly the most connected to the afterlife; out of all of us, she has had the most success when trying to contact and communicate with the dead. We did also have with us a Ouija Board, and even a Demon Board, that we could use if we felt the need. However, those tools are often dangerous in the wrong hands, and can bring things through that are not to be taken lightly. That is especially true of the Demon Board, due to the type of entities it targets. And, given what we knew of the house, we had to proceed with caution.

Lastly, Jenn and I planned to head down to the basement. After all of the assignments were given out, we split up for our respective tasks.

22

INVESTIGATION PART 5

WE ALL MET BACK at HQ after an hour, and each team gave a debriefing of their experiences. Ralph and Jamie went first, relaying what had happened up on the top floor, where they had attempted to make contact with any spirits residing there via an EVP session. They picked a bedroom at random to use, and the questions they asked were standard ones: 'Is there anybody in the room with us?' and 'is there anyone willing to talk?' They were neutral questions designed to evoke a response, but not to anger any spirits that may be near. We simply want an answer, something to build on. Of course, this is difficult if a reply can only be picked up at a later time on a recording, but at least we would then know the room is active, and then return to it and focus on it later.

During the initial bout of questioning, neither Ralph nor Jamie heard any response in real-time, or noticed anything out of the ordinary, save for a palpable and oppressive feeling. Of course, that is hard to quantify and prove as anything paranormal, but I did make a mental note of it, especially since I'd had the same feeling since setting foot inside the house. However, from the glances they kept giving each other during the debrief, I sensed there was more to come.

'It was only when we were getting ready to leave the room that we heard something of note,' Ralph said. 'Three knocks.' He rapped his knuckles on the table in front him in quick succession. 'Just like that. Came from the wall on the far side of the room. It was too clear and precise to be anything other than deliberate, in my view. And it definitely came from inside the room. I'm certain it wasn't noise transference from somewhere else in the house.'

Of course, with George and Ann investigating the ground floor, and Jenn and me in the basement, that should have ruled out the sound coming from anything we were doing. I have seen it before, though, where a sound in an empty house can feel close, only to be coming from someone a few rooms away. However, with two or more floors separating us when it happened, there was no chance of that. Of course, there was one other person present in the house, though I found it doubtful he would have interfered with our investigation. I suppose I cannot fully rule it out, despite Ralph's certainty that the sound came from within the same room. It only happened once, they said, but both Ralph and Jamie are convinced it was paranormal in nature, especially because it happened right when they were leaving the room. Was it a goodbye, or a way to call them back? Given it did not happen again, despite prodding from the two team members, I am swayed to the former.

Ann and George spent their time in the large hall on the ground floor, calling out to any spirits that may have been present. However, whereas the guys on the top floor were using EVP equipment to pick up any response, it was Ann who we hoped would be the conduit here.

I have worked with Ann for a number of years, and I

truly believe she has some level of psychic ability. Many people will scoff at the mere mention of this kind of gift (and I would imagine more than one reader will be rolling their eyes right now), but I have been with Ann when she has channelled the words of the dead, and some of the conversations we have been able to take part in have been fascinating.

After they settled into the great hall, Ann attempted communication. During her debriefing she reported that she'd felt a presence come through almost immediately: a female, whose primary emotion seemed to be fear. Ann asked a series of questions, and found out that this woman was once a house servant who had died in Perron Manor, though the specifics of the woman's death were not revealed. Ann did say, however, that this girl was scared of another presence that currently lived in the house with her.

Ann's findings were indeed interesting, but it was what happened to George that was most surprising. While Ann had been communicating, George claimed he felt a sharp and sudden pain across the back of his neck, like he had been slapped. When Ann checked, she could see what looked to be welts from an actual handprint across George's skin. Thinking quickly, she took a photo with her phone. She showed it to the group during the debrief, and it was unmistakable. Physical contact.

It seemed both teams had had successful experiences, to some degree.

The basement area, where Jenn and I were investigating, was by its very nature a creepy and unsettling place: barefaced stone walls, a cold stone ground, and a heavy and oppressive feel. And it still had the set-up of its past lives, with holding cells in place, minus the doors. I also saw the large, antiquated furnace used to warm the building.

Copper pipes ran from the black iron structure and off into the house to heat it via the circulation of steam. An old and aged system, to be sure, and one that was certainly outdated. Despite that, I was sure it still ran, given there was no other method of heating the house I could see.

There was lighting down in the basement, but we decided to switch off all illumination in order to carry out a vigil.

We had night-vision cameras and sound-recording equipment with us, so I wanted to keep it simple: stay quiet and just see what happened. Asking questions can be a great way to engage spirits, but oftentimes it can pay off just as much to be silent and simply sit in their domain. Sometimes spirits just get curious and seek you out, while other times they get angry at your intrusion and make themselves known.

Whatever entities lurked down there in the basement, it seemed our vigil proved enough of a lure for them to show up.

For about the first thirty minutes, nothing happened, and Jenn and I simply sat in the dark and waited. That can be an anxious thing in itself, and one has to work hard to stop their mind from wandering and turning the most normal and mundane sounds into something they are not. The basement itself is quite a cold and drafty place, and sudden drops in temperature and unexplainable breezes can be sign of paranormal activity. There were a few occasions where I felt the temperature change, but I could not with one-hundred-percent certainty attribute the occurrence to ghosts or spirits (in this instance). My mindset at that time was: unless something happened that was absolutely concrete, I would not consider it as evidence.

When I heard the whisper, I assumed it was Jenn trying to get my attention.

'What is it?' I asked.

'I didn't say anything,' Jenn replied.

Then I heard it again. We both did.

'*David.*'

I instantly tried to communicate and began asking questions of whatever was with us, but the only response I received was the intermittent, almost breathless whisper of my name. Only once did that deviate, and it was the last thing the entity said before it left. There was a single sentence, from a disembodied voice that sounded vaguely female.

'*We... need... you.*'

Thankfully, the conversation was picked up on our audio equipment. Even though some background static made things a little unclear on the recording at times, I believe it is evidence enough to confirm that Jenn and I heard an entity.

After that occurrence, however, we had no further interaction during our vigil.

But considering that was only our first hour of proper investigation work, all three teams certainly turned up some very compelling experiences.

Those proved to be only the beginning.

23

INVESTIGATION PART 6

AFTER OUR EARLY SUCCESS, I was keen to keep the momentum going.

Often, during investigations, you can feel a building energy that coincides with continued activity. It is important to stay on top of that and ride the wave, so to speak. I'd never had such a quick start at a location before (and still haven't to this day), so I wanted to capitalise on it and prove to the spirits that we were ready to listen and communicate. It was already clear to me that there were multiple entities here, which makes sense given the building's history. My hope was that any other spirits present would become curious and also make themselves known to us as well.

Because of that, I decided that the next activity would be to tour the building again, this time in the dark, but we would take our thermographic camera and thermometers with us. The goal was to pick up any rapid fluctuations in temperature, as well as electromagnetic field meters to detect spikes in electromagnetic activity: two telltale signs of spirits. In addition, we would have our night-vision cameras. We still had a lot of time ahead of us, and I felt a leisurely exploration would give us a better understanding of the building and any of its secrets. On top of that, it would give us the best chance to come into contact with as many ghosts as possible.

I decided to start on the top floor, explore that level, then work our way down. Since the top storey was set into the roof space of the building, some of the bedrooms there had sloping ceilings where the roof above ran down to the eaves. That leant these rooms a much more compact and claustrophobia-inducing quality, especially when compared to the more spacious rooms on the lower floors. The windows to the front of the building were cut into the sloping roof, but given how far up we were, they gave great views out to the surrounding grounds. Even at night, thanks to the light of the full moon, we were able to see much of the overgrown and uncared-for gardens that surrounded the property. We could even see out to the boundary walls that enclosed Perron Manor and take in just how big the grounds were.

Though we encountered a few severe and sudden cold spots that were seemingly unexplainable, the top storey offered up little else to us—not even the knocking that Ralph and Jamie had previously heard. It was interesting to explore the bedrooms, however, especially knowing what had happened here in 1982. There was one section of this storey, however, which was closed off and barred by a locked corridor door. I had been under the impression we had the run of the building, so I made a note to speak to Vincent about it the next day, if possible.

We spent a little over an hour up there before moving to the next floor down, though not before Ann felt a sudden presence brush past her and send a jolt of cold through her body. Despite trying to focus in on what may have caused it,

Ann was unable to communicate with anything, so we continued down and started our tour of the next floor.

Like the storey above, there was a thin layer of dust here that indicated years of disuse. In one room, however, we noticed a number of footprints, all of different sizes and shapes. Given only Vincent lived in Perron Manor, and he didn't seem the kind to welcome guests too often, this was slightly strange, but it wasn't something we could state as definitely paranormal. Not unless a footprint formed before our very eyes—which, sadly, did not happen.

There was a bedroom on this storey where we detected another cold spot. This one hit quickly, but this time it remained, not dissipating as those upstairs had done. We set up our recording equipment (both visual and audio) and began to ask questions in the hope of a response. While I didn't initially hear anything, Ralph spoke up and said he was certain he picked up some kind of faint, whispered response. We played back some of the audio equipment, and found that one recorder picked something up very clearly. On it, we could hear the questions we had asked, and then a sudden blast of static, which had been inaudible to us in real-time. But after that burst, we heard a voice. Again, though it had been undetected by us at the time, it was unmistakable on the recording. While it was blanketed in cracking and static itself, we could still pick up a vocalised response, one that sounded pained and struggled, but enough to make out.

The question we had asked first was a simple one. 'Is there anyone listening to us right now.'

The response? '*I. Am. Here.*' And then, there was the distinct sound of a humourless, static-filled laughing.

The next statement came from Jamie. 'If you are here, talk to us. Say something.'

'*You. Are. Not. Listening.*'

Ann was next. 'If anyone is there, know that we can help you.'

The response here was just laughter.

A funny thing about paranormal investigations: despite searching for these rare moments of evidence, when they do occur, we can't help the sense of dread that mixes with the excitement. A feeling of tingling cold runs over your body. Because, despite wanting it so much, when it comes you realise that you don't truly understand it. And probably never will.

At that moment we all felt fear mixed with excitement. But, we pushed on.

24

INVESTIGATION PART 7

GIVEN we now had a method of communication, we acted on it. Our method was to ask a question, pause for a few moments, then replay the audio to see what the answer had been. It proved successful for a time, too.

Ralph asked of the entity, 'Can you tell us what you want?'

Pause. Playback.

'*Him.*'

'Who?' I asked.

'*You.*'

'All of us?' Ann asked. 'Or just David.'

'*Him.*'

Everyone paused and looked in my direction. 'What do you want with me?' I asked.

Pause. Playback.

'*You. Are. Needed. David.*'

'Needed how? I don't understand what you mean.'

But no matter how many times we then recorded dead air and played it back, no response came. It seemed the entity had passed, and we would get no further information from it.

But its message had both intrigued and confused me. *I was needed?* Couple that with the similar, whispered message down in the cellar—*we need you*—and my already considerable interest was well and truly piqued.

The walk around the ground floor and basement levels did not turn up anything this time, but we were still all excited from what we had witnessed so far.

In all my years investigating, I had never had such a frenzied and evidence-rich start. Perron Manor was not disappointing us, giving us plenty to work with. And I couldn't shake the notion that it was somehow deliberate, as well—as if the house was showing off to us.

The hour grew late, and even though investigations usually lasted until the early hours of the morning, we had another full day and night ahead yet, so we decided to turn in for the night. Vincent had arranged a room for each of us, all on the middle floor, and all within close proximity to each other. Once we retired for the night, each member would keep a night-vision-capable video recorder with them, as well as an audio recorder. Just because we were splitting up to sleep, didn't mean the investigation had to cease completely.

During the night, most members of the group remained undisturbed. However, come the next morning, Ann, Jamie, and myself all had experiences to recount.

25

INVESTIGATION PART 8

IT WAS a little past seven in the morning when we all wandered down to the HQ area for breakfast.

I was feeling a little off, given what had happened the previous night, and the group could sense it, immediately asking me if I was okay. First, however, I wanted to know if any of the others had had anything happen to them.

Jamie spoke first.

'I heard more of that knocking again. Woke me up at about three in the morning. It was a rapping on the door, in bursts of three. Obviously, I looked out into the hall, but no one was there. So I settled back down to try and get some sleep, but it happened again. Kept doing it, too. Scared the shit out of me. And every time it happened, it was just as I felt myself relaxing and falling asleep again. It was like something was just tormenting me.'

'That explains why you look like shit,' Jenn said with a chuckle.

'Anyone else experience anything?' I asked.

Ann raised her hand. 'I had a visitor,' she said. 'I remember waking up, funnily enough at about three in the morning as well, and saw a dark presence standing at the foot of my bed.'

'Dark presence?' Jenn asked. 'Care to elaborate on that?'

'Well, I felt it just as much as saw it. The shadows around it seemed to almost swim, outlining a humanoid shape. It just stood and watched, but did not want to communicate.'

I saw Jenn give an eyeroll, which thankfully Ann missed. It is fair to say that Jenn was not quite a believer when it came to Ann's gifts, and there had always been a slight animosity.

Ann went on. 'It stayed with me for a little while, before dissipating. There isn't much more to tell.'

'Did you get it on video?' Jenn asked—a fair question.

Ann shook her head. 'I just felt that the entity would have disappeared sooner, had I tried that.'

'Of course it would have,' Jenn said.

'What about you, David?' Ralph interjected, which I knew was just as much to avoid an argument between the two girls as it was genuine interest. 'Anything to tell?'

I nodded. 'Yeah, as a matter of fact, I do.' I took a breath, recalling what had happened the previous night. 'Again, it was about three in the morning, same as you two. I was woken up by something shaking me. I have to say, I panicked a little, as it was quite violent. I got my nerves under control and looked around the room, but could see nothing. It was then I heard the whispering. A female voice. Again, it was saying "you are needed" over and over. By the time I got my audio equipment out, the whispering had stopped.'

'Not the first time we've heard something like that about you,' Ralph said. 'That you are "needed." I think the house has focused in on you specifically.'

'Well,' Ann cut in, 'I think it could be both David *and* myself. I've had quite a few experiences, too. Maybe it's focusing on both of us.'

Jenn ignored Ann. 'We need to take that seriously, David. If it *has* zeroed in on you, we know that can be dangerous.'

She was right. When a spirit focuses solely on one person in a group, ignoring all others, often it means that entity harbours some kind of malevolence to the target. I didn't think that was the case here, however, as to me it seemed more like a message. And I intended to find out what it meant.

26

INVESTIGATION PART 9

AFTER BREAKFAST, we were paid a visit by Vincent Bell. He walked into our HQ room dressed in blue pyjamas and a dark burgundy robe that looked like it needed a good wash. He pointed a bony finger at me.

'I'd like a word with you,' Vincent said, then turned and left. I raised my eyebrows at the others, but then followed him out of the room. He led me to the library, which was an impressive space with bookshelves completely covering two of the walls, giving the area a feeling of grandeur and history.

Vincent sat down on an old, ornate recliner and looked up at me, but he didn't say anything.

'You wanted to talk to me?' I asked, trying to get things moving. I remember his response very clearly. The whole conversation, in fact.

'I did,' he said, with a nod that was almost solemn. 'There's a few things you need to know about this place... and about me. I don't get a chance to talk to people often, so it don't come easy to me anymore. I'm sorry if I've been short with you so far. But I know you'll believe me about this place. That's why you're here, after all. You believe there is more to life after we pass, don't you?'

I nodded. 'Yes.'

'And *that's* why I decided to let you in. I know you won't judge. This house will certainly give you the proof you've been looking for. It's always been active, for as long as I've been here, anyway.'

'So... you're saying you believe the house is haunted?' I asked, and Vincent gave a slow nod.

'It is. I came here after Marcus Blackwater invited me to move in. He was the former owner, and an old friend.'

'I know of him,' I said. 'To be honest, I know quite a bit about the history of the house in general. And I also know that Marcus left it to you after what happened in 1982.'

'Aye,' Vincent said. 'Halloween. Lot of people know about that night. But none of them know what *really* happened.'

'But you do,' I said, pulling up a chair and sitting down. 'You were there. You and your family were the only ones that got out.'

'That's true.'

'Well... would you mind telling me what happened that night? I've always been fascinated by it.'

Vincent paused. He seemed to be struggling with something, obviously unsure. Perhaps it was an issue of trust. Whatever his reticence, however, he eventually reached a favourable decision.

'Alright,' he said. 'This is what I know.'

27

INVESTIGATION PART 10

SOME OF THIS next section may sound a little like a recap, given I've covered the night in 1982 earlier in the book. But, I am recounting what Vincent told me next so that you can see where much of my understanding of the tragic night—and the house under Marcus Blackwater's ownership in general—comes from.

Vincent started at the beginning, sharing from when he first moved into the house. He said that Marcus had always been a good friend, and the two met at university, with Vincent being impressed he'd found someone with even more of a love of the occult than himself.

He had long been aware of Perron Manor, as Marcus had mentioned it many times during their friendship, and learned that Marcus always hoped to inherit what he thought was 'the most haunted house in the country.'

So, when the time came and Vincent got the call, he jumped at the chance to move in, dropping everything else he had going on in life to do so.

I'm not certain where Vincent's interest in the occult

originally came from, but given my own interests I certainly wasn't going to judge, and so I didn't ask.

Vincent went on to tell me a little about Marcus Blackwater. He talked about Marcus in glowing terms, at first: friendly, warm, and charming. But Marcus was also a man used to getting what he wanted, Vincent said, and there was a certain single-minded focus beneath his welcoming exterior.

My host then told me about the first year of living in the Manor, where he had started to witness activity for himself. It was small at first, the odd knocking or whispering—scary, but exciting.

In addition, as each day passed Vincent said he noticed a change in Marcus. When Vincent's friend revealed his plans to turn the building into a hotel, Vincent had been shocked. Marcus didn't need the money, given what he had inherited, so it didn't make sense to take on a burden or a business like that. But Marcus could not be swayed. Fortunately, Vincent knew a person who could help—his sister, Rita. She, along with her husband and daughter, came to live in the Manor with them, and they all got to work getting the Blackwater Hotel ready for business.

The new arrivals soon began to sense something 'odd' about the house, and Vincent said he started to feel guilty about bringing them in, though he swore that he never for one second imagined anything could or would actually hurt them.

Things progressed, business was 'okay,' and then Marcus dropped another bombshell of an idea. A way to boost publicity, he'd said. A free haunted weekend for people of good standing in the local area.

Again, Vincent couldn't understand the rationale behind

it, but Marcus would not be swayed. So it was arranged. And it happened.

As the first day of the event grew closer, Vincent said that Marcus' personality changed even more. The man was obsessed with the weekend event they were planning, to an unhealthy degree. And that was, Vincent said, the first time he realised he should have spoken up in protest. But he didn't.

So, the first day of the event arrived. Guests funnelled in, and all was well to begin with. But Vincent claims he felt something bubbling beneath the surface. Claimed that the house was 'stirring,' and he had an unshakable feeling that Marcus was behind it all, setting something up. What that was, exactly, Vincent didn't know.

After the first night, some guests claimed to have had 'experiences,' and Vincent recalls that one woman decided she was leaving for good. He claims she was white as a sheet the next morning, and said someone had been standing outside of her ground-floor window during the night. She could see him through the glass, standing stationary while he watched her, with a pale face and blank expression. She apparently ran to a friend's room and stayed there until morning. After that, however, she was so shaken, her weekend stay was over.

Vincent noted that Marcus was strangely absent during most of the Saturday, hiding away somewhere. And Vincent also stated that he had a growing sense of dread building inside of him, something that he could not quite place. Eventually, he found Marcus and confronted him, asking his friend what was really going on. Vincent claims he felt Marcus was perhaps dabbling with some unknown occult magic or the like, and rather than this event being a marketing ploy, it was actually serving a different purpose for the owner of the building. But Marcus was abrupt with Vincent, telling his friend to simply leave if he wasn't happy with the way things were.

And that was that. Marcus walked away, and Vincent never saw his friend again.

Though the rest of the day, and the following night, produced an increase in reported incidents, it wasn't until Sunday night that things escalated to unimaginable levels.

Vincent recalls how that night he wanted to be away from the hustle and bustle of the event, and retired to his room early, hoping to get some sleep. It was early in the morning—about one—when he was woken by the sound of screaming.

After quickly getting dressed, he left his room to see chaos in the corridor outside. People were panicking and running around in terror. Vincent remembered terrible noises as well. Inhuman sounds. And he saw things that were hard to put into words. Terrifying beings that were causing chaos. Vincent even claims to have seen people pulled into the very walls around them.

The old man stated he didn't remember too much more, and didn't really know how he and his family escaped that night. His next memory was of standing on the grass outside of the house, as the screaming started to die down and the sound of police sirens got closer.

It was only in the weeks that followed that Vincent found out he was the inheritor of Perron Manor, with Marcus—who had been found dead—having added Vincent as sole benefactor in his will only a few months prior.

'But why would he do that?' I asked. 'It seems strange that he would have added you before the Halloween weekend and then take his life like that. It all seems premeditated.'

'I agree,' Vincent replied. 'I figure he wanted someone around to keep Perron Manor going.'

'But why take his own life?'

'Pretty sure he had his reasons,' Vincent said. 'For one, I feel that there is part of him that continues on here, among the dead that still remain.'

'So he *wanted* to be trapped here?'

Vincent shrugged. 'Not sure what his plan was. I can tell you this, though... I don't think it's finished yet.'

'Can I ask you one more thing?' I said, feeling the welcome conversation was, unfortunately, drawing to a close. 'Why did you really change your mind with me? Why let me in here now?'

'Like I said, I think you'll treat the house with the respect it deserves. And it's also nice to hear things in this house for once, knowing they're normal sounds actually made by the living.'

I could understand that. 'It must be hard living here alone, and doing it for so long. Why not leave?'

'Because if this place is left empty, it draws in the innocent. I decided long ago to dedicate my life to keeping people away as much as possible. You and your friends are a rare exception, so don't waste the opportunity.'

I wanted to keep talking, to ask him what it had been like living alone in this place for all those years. From the history I'd uncovered, anyone who resided here for any significant length of time had always come under the influence of the house, but Vincent seemed to be the exception. I also wanted to ask him about the area on the top floor that seemed to be closed off.

However, there was to be no more conversing. Vincent

stood up and left. 'Carry on with your investigation, Mr. Ritter,' he said before going. 'And, as I said, make the most of it.'

28

INVESTIGATION PART 11

AFTER BRIEFING the team about what Vincent told me, we got to work reviewing footage from the stationary cameras that had been running overnight. Again, we hit paydirt, capturing something on the camera in the foyer.

On the footage—which was bathed in green hue of night-vision—we could see a faint shadow walking down the stairs at 3.05 am. It isn't much more than that, but was nonetheless very easy to see. The humanoid form stops directly outside of the door to our HQ and... just stands there. Eventually, after about two minutes, the shape slowly fades away to nothing. We must have watched that sequence on repeat three or four times that morning, and countless times since. For me, it is indisputable proof.

There was nothing else recorded of note that we could find, so we got to work with the day's investigation, where we decided to split it up into three main activities. The morning would consist of a 'free period,' where everyone was encouraged to follow their own impulses as they saw fit, as long as no one went off on their own. We would then break for lunch, before moving on to trying a séance. In the evening we would try something a little more extreme, but only if we felt it necessary, given we'd already had great results so far.

The free time in the morning did not yield much in the way of results. I again visited the top storey and saw that frustrating locked door which closed us off to 'something' up there. I considered finding Vincent and asking him for a key, but figured he'd been gracious enough so far in letting us in here in the first place, so pushing our welcome wouldn't be wise.

When we reassembled for lunch, the only person with anything to report was Jenn, who said that she and Jamie had heard a loud banging on the ground floor room they were in. It came in a swift burst of three. She also claims to have heard a faint whisper of 'help me.' But despite investigating further, the pair found nothing else.

After we refuelled ourselves at lunch, it was time for the séance. Now, I was well aware before we started that the chances of success were slim. Though I do believe Ann has some sensitivity, I do not think she is a full psychic. Because of that, getting results with a séance would be difficult, since it takes considerable power to connect and communicate with the otherworld for any sustained length of time. Still, Ann was keen to try it, and I felt it was certainly worth a shot.

We chose the great hall on the ground floor as the location, and we all sat down around the table. Normally, these things are carried out at night in darkened rooms, but the best we could do was draw the heavy curtains closed. It had already crossed my mind that maybe we should swap the séance to later that evening, but in truth I wanted that time clear for the other thing we had planned.

We all sat around the large table, with Ann at the head. I

could tell Jenn was less than enthused during the experiment, as she doubted Ann's abilities. Thankfully, she didn't say anything, at least at first. Then we all joined hands (Ralph and Jamie having to lean over the width of the table to do so, since they were sitting opposite one another) and settled in. Silence fell, and then Ann began to speak, asking if anyone was present.

There was nothing. No response at all. We tried for over an hour, and just when I had decided the whole thing was a bust, Ann began to twitch.

'What's wrong?' I asked.

'I feel something,' she replied. The twitch progressed to a shake. I saw Jenn roll her eyes, but I felt like it might be something genuine.

'Ann?' I asked. 'What's happening?'

She suddenly stopped, her eyes went wide, and her jaw fell a little slack. 'I hear someone speaking to me,' she said.

We all waited.

'It is a young boy,' Ann said, her wide eyes staring off into space. 'He says he is looking for someone.'

I immediately thought of the boy who had gone missing back when the house was an orphanage—whose mother had sworn she had seen him up here in this house. I was about to ask who it was the boy was searching for, but Ann went on. 'He's looking for his sister. Asking if we have seen her.' Ann shook her head slowly, then responded to the young boy. 'No, dear, we have not seen her. What is her name?'

Then, I heard a loud screech and we all jumped. It was Jenn, jumping to her feet, and breaking the circle in the process. The sudden noise had been her chair sliding across the hard floor.

'This is garbage!'

'Sit down, Jenn,' I said, but she didn't comply.

'I'm sorry, David, but look where we are. Look at the place we are investigating. *Finally*. How long have we waited? I don't think we should be wasting our precious time here on a charade like this.'

Ann took offence, and claimed Jenn had ruined the experiment. Frustratingly, the séance then ground to a sudden halt as bickering broke out between the two women.

'Enough!' I yelled, and rose to my feet as well. 'Jenn, you had no right to ruin the séance. If you didn't want to be involved, you didn't have to be.'

She didn't answer, just stood with her arms folded across her chest, looking angry.

'We can carry on,' Ann insisted. 'If we start again, I'm sure we can reach the boy once more.'

I looked to the others, and saw Ralph shake his head. 'I'm not sure this is a good fit for us,' he said diplomatically. 'Séances aren't exactly something we can prove one way or the other. And we are here for actual evidence. Unless this conversation—and I don't mean any offence by this, Ann—leads to more than just Ann talking with a spirit, then we need to move on, since we'd have no physical proof.'

Jamie agreed. George said nothing.

Ralph had a point, even if Jenn had gone about the whole thing the wrong way.

'Fine,' I said. 'But does that change what we had planned later? Do we give up on the Demon Board?'

After a few moments of silence, Ralph spoke. 'I don't think so. We *know* that can lead to results. However, we should be asking ourselves if it is safe to use something like that *here*?'

We debated it for a short while, but decided the potential rewards outweighed the risks.

So, we spent the rest of the night investigating, and running smaller experiments.

Compared to the previous day, we were met with precious little activity, and this only reinforced that the house would show us things only when it wanted to. It made me a little concerned that the Demon Board would fail.

My concern should have been for just how well it would succeed.

29

INVESTIGATION PART 12

DEMON BOARDS ARE A LESSER-KNOWN version of a Ouija Board, only much more dangerous. As the name would suggest, where a Ouija Board contacts the spirits of the dead, the Demon Board contacts demonic entities, hence the danger involved.

They are not very common, which is a good thing, in my eyes, and they need to be handled with care. With these boards, you are not asking to speak to the deceased, and the entities that may come through are malevolent by nature, so one must be both experienced and trained in the use of such equipment.

Fortunately, I have plenty of experience in using them, and own one of the few in existence. It took years to hunt down, and set me back a pretty penny. While it is a tool in our arsenal, it is something we use only on occasion.

While we had no evidence that there was a demonic presence in the house, we agreed it was an educated guess to assume there was, given the long and tragic history. Simple spirits of the dead were unlikely to be responsible for such a feat.

We decided to try and communicate with whatever was behind the power this building had, if there was any such an entity.

I guessed the best place to do that was the lowest and darkest location in the house, a place demons are known to dwell.

The basement level.

While we set up (which consisted of placing camera and audio equipment, as well as putting down a small, portable table to rest the board on and accompanying chairs), we made sure the lights down there were all on. Even bathed in the dull, yellow lighting, the basement was a creepy place. And I couldn't help but stare at the furnace, knowing what had happened to the young lad many years ago.

By the time we were ready, it was approaching one in the morning, so we sat around the table and laid down the board. On this particular Demon Board, there is an etching of a goat's head in the centre, and its outline—with horns splayed upwards and ears splayed down—form the shape of a pentagram. Around this picture are concentric circles, getting progressively bigger, and the letters of the alphabet we would use to communicate are laid out in circular shape between them. There is a symbol for 'Yes' in the top left-hand corner, and a symbol representing 'No' in the top right, and at the bottom corners are the words 'Hello' and 'Goodbye.'

I set the planchette down, then looked to everyone.

'Are we ready?'

We were. So, we killed the main lights—leaving us with only torchlight—and each laid a light finger on the planchette.

'Is there anybody there?'

30

INVESTIGATION PART 13

As with the séance, nothing happened at first, and our questions and calls went unanswered.

However, after a while I again asked if anyone was there, and we finally felt the planchette move from 'Hello,' and hover over the word 'Yes.'

We all looked at each other, every member sure the others played no part in any subtle movements of the marker. And we all immediately felt the temperature drop. It was instantaneous, and our breaths were visible, hanging in the air. I felt a prick of fear work its way up my spine.

This was it.

I got my bearings quickly, and asked for the demon's name, knowing we had to find out who we were dealing with, as names had great power over demonic forces.

The planchette moved over to the letter P. Then to A. Then to Z, then U, Z, and finally U again. After ceasing its movements momentarily, the planchette then slipped from all our grasps, shot away from the board, and skittered across the floor.

I heard someone let out a yelp of fright.

'Stay calm,' I ordered, though I definitely didn't feel calm myself. I knew of the name the board had spelt out, and we needed to get the planchette back quickly in order to close the link. We began frantically searching for it, but then a scream, this one loud and terrified, drew my attention. It was Ann, and she was pointing her torch to the far corner of the basement.

We could all see what she had picked up. It was a young girl, peeking out from behind one of the cell walls. Her skin was grey and mottled, and her eyes milky-white.

This was certainly no demon. It was a spirit, I guessed, and the most clearly visible I had ever witnessed in my life. I quickly brought up my handheld camera to capture it, but just as I did the lens at the front blew out with a crash.

'Who are you?' Jenn asked.

A soulless cackle was the response as she ducked from view. Eventually, we found enough courage to go over to where she had been standing, but found the cell empty. Still, the cold in the basement was getting worse. Then, we heard an inhuman voice echo all around us. I swear, I have never known terror like in that moment.

'You. Are. Needed. David. Return here. Help another in need.'

Another message. I know how this all sounds, but I swear it is true. Then, from another corner of the space we heard a goat bleat, but there was no animal in sight. A dull banging started to erupt from the walls around us, as if scores of people were slapping against the brick and stone.

'We need to go,' Ralph said, and I could hear the terror in his voice. When I swung around, my flashlight caught the briefest glimpse of something in its beam. Not enough to make out exactly what it was, and I couldn't find it again when swaying my beam around frantically, but I saw enough to know it wasn't human. Whatever it was, the entity was jet black, with long limbs, and it skittered out of my light.

I felt myself hyperventilate as my fear levels rose. Ralph was right. This was above us.

But we needed to stop what was happening first.

'Find the planchette,' I instructed. 'We need to cut the link before we go, otherwise whatever it is could follow any one of us.'

We searched desperately as the terrible noises continued around us. At one point I saw that little girl again, and again she was peeking at me from around the corner of a wall. But just like the last time, she vanished after we closed in. I heard her giggle.

We were being toyed with.

Eventually, George found the planchette, and we again gathered around the Demon Board. We all set our fingers on the marker, moved it over 'Goodbye,' and then all said the word as well. Just as we did, I looked up, and swear I saw some kind of twisted, demonic-looking face just behind Jenn, eyeing me wildly, with a long, snake-like tongue lolling from its mouth. It had black skin, wide, yellow eyes, and features that looked like melted wax.

Later, Jenn told me once we finished that I screamed wildly for over five minutes until the others calmed me down, though I don't remember that at all (not that I disbelieve her, of course). The thing I do remember, however, was the temperature rising again, and feeling lighter, like an oppressive weight had gone.

Now, in no way am I implying that we had somehow cleansed Perron Manor from whatever resides there, but we certainly reversed whatever we'd started with the Demon Board.

We again put on the lights, packed up our gear, and

moved back upstairs to HQ. I could tell that every single member of the group was shaken—rightfully so—and exhausted.

We decided to forgo any more investigative work because, as Jamie put it, 'I don't think I really want to see any more tonight.'

There was a palpable sense of fear and exhaustion that ran through the group. We decided to bring things to a close, but that night we slept in twos, rather than having a room each to ourselves.

Thankfully, nothing else happened, but as a whole we barely slept a wink. The morning brought with it an end to our investigation, and we packed everything up. It was a slow process, hindered by the utter exhaustion we all felt.

Before we left, Vincent wandered in to see us, and me especially.

'Finished?'

'I believe so, sir. The agreement was two nights, so I'd say we got what we asked for. Thank you.'

'Good. Now pack up your stuff and go. And don't come back.'

I raised my eyebrows. Just yesterday, the man had seemed to soften and open up, but now he was back to being the inhospitable old crank he had been upon our arrival.

'Okay,' I replied, not sure what else to say. 'We'll leave, of course, but would you not consider letting us return one day to—'

'You won't ever come back!' he snapped. 'Not as long as I'm alive. Now fuck off, the lot of you!'

And he strode off. And that was the rather abrupt end of our investigation of Perron Manor.

AFTERWORD

That is the story of Perron Manor.

At least, the story so far. Because I have no doubt there is more to come from that house.

I hope my research into its history has been interesting, and has given you a little more appreciation for the impressive past the Manor has, as well as the terrible events that have befallen it.

Every word I have written is true, and it remains to this day the most active location I have ever been to. It yielded much in the way of evidence, even if, sadly, every piece of recording equipment failed while we were down in the basement with the Demon Board.

I cannot forget the messages that were left for me by the spirits there. That I'm somehow *needed*. I still don't fully know what that means, but I don't plan on giving up trying to get back there. Vincent has ignored all my requests since then, but I will keep trying. Perseverance worked once before, so I have to believe it will work again.

Perron Manor is important to me. It has confirmed my belief in the afterlife.

However, it also brings with it a certain fear, because it is clear there are certain entities residing there that are definitely malevolent in nature.

Perhaps Archie Reynolds put it best.

'Life after death isn't necessarily a good thing. Certainly not for the souls trapped in that house. I firmly believe they are doomed to suffer there forever.'

I'm not sure if the souls trapped there are suffering or not, but I know that I have to do everything I can to help them.

And, because of that, I am certain I will once again step foot in Perron Manor. I won't rest until I do.

—*David Ritter, Paranormal Investigator, 2018.*

HAUNTED: PERRON MANOR

Now you know the history, dive into the *real* horror.

Haunted: Perron Manor
Book 1 in the Haunted Series.

Sisters Sarah and Chloe inherit a house they could never have previously dreamed of owning. It seems too good to be true.

Shortly after they move in, however, the siblings start to notice strange things: horrible smells, sudden drops in temperature, as well as unexplainable sounds and feelings of being watched.

All of that is compounded when they find a study upstairs, filled with occult items and a strange book written in Latin.

Their experiences grow more frequent and more terrifying, building towards a heart-stopping climax where the sisters come face to face with the evil behind Perron Manor. Will they survive and save their very souls?

Buy Haunted: Perron Manor now.

OTHER BOOKS BY LEE MOUNTFORD

The Supernatural Horror Collection
  The Demonic
  The Mark
  Forest of the Damned

The Extreme Horror Collection
  Horror in the Woods
  Tormented
  The Netherwell Horror

Haunted Series
  Inside Perron Manor (Book 0)
  Haunted: Perron Manor (Book 1)
  Haunted: Devil's Door (Book 2)
  Haunted: Purgatory (Book 3)
  Haunted: Possession (Book 4)
  Haunted: Mother Death (Book 5)
  Haunted: Asylum (Book 6)
  Haunted: Hotel (Book 7)
  Haunted: Catacombs (Book 8)
  Haunted: End of Days (Book 9)

Darkfall Series
  Darkfall: Deathborn (Book 1)
  Darkfall: Shadows of the Deep (Book 2)
  Darkfall: Crimson Dawn (Book 3)

ABOUT THE AUTHOR

Lee Mountford is a horror author from the North-East of England. His first book, Horror in the Woods, was published in May 2017 to fantastic reviews, and his follow-up book, The Demonic, achieved Best Seller status in both Occult Horror and British Horror categories on Amazon.

He is a lifelong horror fan, much to the dismay of his amazing wife, Michelle, and his work is available in ebook, print and audiobook formats.

In August 2017 he and his wife welcomed their first daughter, Ella, into the world. In May 2019, their second daughter, Sophie, came along. Michelle is hoping the girls don't inherit their father's love of horror, but Lee has other ideas...

For more information
www.leemountford.com
leemountford01@googlemail.com

ACKNOWLEDGMENTS

Thanks first to my amazing Beta Reader Team, who have greatly helped me polish and hone this book:

James Bacon
Christine Brlevic
John Brooks
Carrie-Lynn Cantwell
Karen Day
Doreene Fernandes
Jenn Freitag
Ursula Gillam
Clayton Hall
Tammy Harris
Emily Haynes
Dorie Heriot
Lemmy Howells
Lucy Hughes
Dawn Keate
Valerie Palmer
Leanne Pert
Justin Read
Nicola Jayne Smith
Sara Walker
Sharon Watret

Also, thanks to my editor, Josiah Davis (http://www.jdbookservices.com) for such an amazing job as always.

The cover was supplied by Debbie at The Cover Collection. (http://www.thecovercollection.com). I cannot recommend their work enough.

And the last thank you, as always, is the most important—to my amazing family. My wife, Michelle, and my daughters, Ella and Sophie: thank you for everything. You three are my world.

Copyright © 2020 by Lee Mountford

All rights reserved.

No part of this book may be reproduced in any form or by any electronic or mechanical means, including information storage and retrieval systems, without written permission from the author, except for the use of brief quotations in a book review.

❀ Created with Vellum

Printed in Great Britain
by Amazon